NOONDAY AND NIGHT

Gladys Mitchell

NOONDAY AND NIGHT

LONDON

MICHAEL JOSEPH

First published in Great Britain by Michael Joseph Ltd
52 Bedford Square, London WC1B 3EF
1977

ISBN 0 7181 1517 1

Printed and bound in Great Britain by
REDWOOD BURN LIMITED
Trowbridge and Esher

To my niece
ENID MITCHELL
in admiration of her sculpture

CHAPTER 1

Pottery and Porcelain

The invitation to dinner was accompanied by two slightly unusual requests. One was that Dame Beatrice would bring another woman with her, preferably one who was interested in ceramics; the other was that she would also bring her two blue-dash English delftware dishes, chargers which had been made round about AD 1640, although whether in London or Bristol was uncertain.

One sentence in Basil Honfleur's letter appeared to explain this otherwise curious request. 'I've recently become possessed of a particularly fine early nineteenth century Welsh dresser, and I would love to see how your two pieces look on it compared with some which my crockery scout Vittorio has managed to pick up for me.'

This, Dame Beatrice thought, was an elliptical way of indicating that, if her pieces looked well on his shelves, there would be an offer to purchase them. After the dinner, she supposed, the company would adjourn to the kitchen and the dishes would be put on display. Then would follow a bargaining battle between the knowledgeable woman Dame Beatrice would have brought with her if she could think of anybody suitable, and Vittorio (whoever he was), to fix upon the price to be offered.

Dame Beatrice was not particularly attached to her delftware, which had been left her by a distant relative for whom she had

had little affection. It was neither uncommon nor, she supposed, very valuable. She considered it, in fact, to be rather ugly and, compared with her collection of Sèvres porcelain (actually made in the factory at Vincennes before that was transferred to Sèvres itself), extremely crude. One charger was decorated with a figure on horseback which might or might not represent Prince Rupert; the other showed Adam, Eve and the serpent, Adam chastely upholstered in an apron of fig leaves which appeared to depend upon faith alone for its support, Eve content apparently with her Godiva-like mantle of hair. The serpent, writhing down from a loaded fruit-tree, was focusing its attention upon the apple (or whatever) which was being passed from hand to hand by the other two.

'Take Conradda Mendel,' said Laura Gavin, the secretary, when Dame Beatrice showed her Basil Honfleur's letter. 'They've got another thing in common besides an interest in antiques.'

Laura meant by this that both Honfleur and Miss Mendel had once upon a time attended Dame Beatrice's clinic for psychiatric treatment. It had happened, Dame Beatrice remembered, that she had arranged for the decorators to take over her Kensington house where, at that time, her clinic was held, and so she had fitted up a room on the first floor of her Hampshire residence, the Stone House on the edge of the New Forest, and for a few weeks she had carried on her work there. Those whose commitments did not permit them to attend had been referred to another psychiatrist in London and their case histories handed over to him.

Both Honfleur and Conradda had found the change of venue acceptable and, in Honfleur's case, convenient, since it saved him the longer journey to London. He and Conradda had met at the Stone House on one or two occasions, owing either to unavoidable delays on the road or to the vagaries of the train services, and had taken tea together at the Stone House.

Honfleur had been in a Commando unit during the war;

Conradda had suffered persecution under the Nazis. He was now well settled in an occupation which suited him. Conradda was a dealer in antiques who did a little very high-class pawn-broking on the side, although her clientèle was not subjected to the sight of three golden balls above her extremely exclusive Mayfair premises. It was she who had found the Sèvres for Dame Beatrice and it was her proud contention that the only collection which could match it was that at Waddesdon, the former home of Baron Ferdinand de Rothschild.

Dame Beatrice knew that this statement on Conradda's part was a wild distortion of the truth, but she treasured her pieces and no servant was ever allowed to put a finger on them. She had seen Miss Alice de Rothschild's collection in the enormous French-Renaissance-style mansion administered nowadays by the National Trust and had admired but did not covet it, and she had treated Conradda's contention with mirth.

'Conradda Mendel?' she said, in answer to Laura's suggestion. 'I thought perhaps you yourself would like to come. It may be a dinner well worth eating, and you would do better justice to it than I shall.'

'No,' said Laura. 'Reading between the lines, this Honfleur wants to get his hooks on to your dishes. You take Conradda and watch the fur fly when she and this Italian really go into a clinch over the price. If it isn't an impertinent question, shall you consider selling?'

'Oh, yes, I expect so, if Mr Honfleur wants them; I don't at all care for the chargers.'

'Me neither, as Fowler would hardly permit us to say. Shall I ring up Conradda, then? They do actually know one another, don't they?'

'Yes, they met here at the Stone House when I had that room next to mine converted into a consulting room for a while.'

Conradda, apprised over the telephone by Laura of the probable reason for the invitation, accepted it with alacrity, but warned her that if Vittorio was also 'in the business, although I do not know anyone of that name,' he would know her by repute if not by sight.

'I might call myself Leah Cohen, don't you think?' she suggested. Laura said firmly that Dame Beatrice would not like that.

'Besides, Honfleur knows you, even if this Italian does not. Anyway, we mustn't go in for subterfuge,' she said. 'Not ethical.'

'Business precautions, that is all,' said the Jewess. 'Will it be a good dinner? I do not insist upon kosher food.'

Vittorio was a tiny, monkey-like little man, sinuous and very thin. When the introduction was made, it seemed, surprisingly, that Conradda's name meant nothing at all to the olive-skinned, shifty-eyed Italian: if he was the expert he seemed to be — there was no doubt, from the conversation over cocktails and again at the table, that he certainly knew a great deal about antiques of all kinds — it was odd, to say the least, that he had not heard of Conradda, who was a well-known figure at all the important auctions, besides being a collector in her own right. There was no obvious reason for him to dissemble. Although Conradda could drive a hard bargain, she was known to be scrupulously fair in her trade dealings, even refusing to take advantage of the ignorant beyond what she called 'my pickings, because I have had to pay for my knowledge on my way up, so only right I should expect just a small profit, don't you think?'

Dame Beatrice, who could always keep several streams of thought, unconnected with one another, in her mind at one and the same time, covertly studied Vittorio while conversing amiably with her host on the subject of his business. Honfleur was in charge of the main booking office of a motor-coach company which ran extended tours, as they were called in the official brochure, to the various scenic or historic parts of England, Wales, Scotland and Eire, and also to France, Germany, Austria and northern Italy. Part of his job (and the pleasantest part, he explained to Dame Beatrice), was to leave his office on occasion in order to follow up the various tours and report upon the hotels which the coaches used for overnight stops *en route.*

He was a short, powerfully-built man of about fifty-five and gave the impression of being vigorous and capable. Dame Beatrice, however, having once had him as a patient, knew a good deal about him. He always sent her a Christmas card, but beyond that their acquaintanceship had not made any progress until she had received the unexpected invitation to dinner. This, however, explained itself because it was clear, she thought, that it was her delftware and not her company which was important to him.

While she was listening to his description of a trip he had made that summer to two Continental hotels on which his firm desired a confidential report since there had been adverse criticism of them from some of the passengers, she heard the tiny, olive-skinned Vittorio say to Conradda Mendel,

'You have a personal interest in ceramics?'

'Oh, I run a general little junk-shop,' she replied. 'All is grist to my mill, not only ceramics.'

'You work in London?'

'I also have a place in Oxford, but the students, they have no money for nice pictures and china nowadays. I think I shall sell up and perhaps go to Bath.'

'I wonder whether there is much money in Bath, either? There might be some nice things to pick up there, though, which you could sell in London. Do you have good connections?'

'I welcome any customers who come in, that is all.'

'I suppose one has to do that if one keeps a shop. I myself am a free-lance, following my nose and picking up here a little something, there a little something else. I have clients, people who tell me what they want and who trust my judgement. You are not interested particularly in ceramics, you say?'

'That takes specialised knowledge.'

Dame Beatrice could have explained that a knowledge of ceramics *was* Conradda's particular line of country. However, she did not avail herself of the opportunity, but left such a confession to Conradda herself, if she chose to make it, which apparently she did not. Dame Beatrice concluded that such a claim, in Conradda's opinion, since there might be a chance of selling the delftware dishes to Honfleur, might be bad for business. She was secretly amused by this thought and looked forward to being an observer of the various ploys which would be involved when Greek met Greek, or, in this case, when clever Jewess skirmished with wily Italian.

'I rather wish you were more interested in pottery, because, as a matter of fact,' said Honfleur, who had finished his description of a new coach he had just put on the road, 'I wouldn't be averse to parting with one or two of my own pieces, if you would care to look them over, Miss Mendel.'

'Oh, but, now, now!' cried Vittorio. 'After I go to all that trouble to collect them for you? You break my heart when you say you are willing to part with them.'

'Well, it's that Welsh dresser I bought,' explained his client. 'It will only hold just so much, if the dishes are to be displayed to advantage. We have some duplicates . . .'

'No, never! I do not buy duplicates for you. Those which are something alike are of different years. Look at the marks on the back! You speak of your Bristol delft, no doubt, but consider and do not be so hasty to part with your treasures.'

'Oh, well,' said Honfleur pacifically, 'after dinner we'll take the pieces down and have a look at the date-marks. I had no idea you'd be so upset at the thought of selling. I might even give one or two of the dishes to you for your own collection. How about that?'

'Very kind. We shall see when the time comes.' Vittorio did not sound at all enthusiastic, Dame Beatrice thought. She changed the subject to that of the ex-Emperor Charles V and his Swiss palace full of clocks and this topic lasted the company for the rest of the meal.

After coffee had been served amid conversation which did not include the subject of ceramics, an adjournment was made to the kitchen. Honfleur's was not a large house, but all the rooms were spacious, the kitchen not less so than the rest.

'I call it the kitchen, but, of course, no cooking is done in it,' said the host. 'Most of my food comes in ready cooked from outside, except for my breakfast. I go to the *Regal* for that, and quite often, if I'm not entertaining at home, I go there for dinner too. Well, what do you think of the set-up?'

'Remarkable,' said Dame Beatrice, gazing around at the furnishings. 'Most interesting.'

There were two immediately impressive objects in the room. One was a tremendous kitchen table, but even more noticeable, because of its loaded shelves, was the magnificent Welsh dresser. On its three shelves, the lowest of which was formed of a dozen very small drawers, each with its rounded wooden knob, were arranged Honfleur's collection of plates and dishes.

'The dresser is large, but not large enough. That's my trouble. There isn't room enough on the dresser itself to display the whole collection,' he said.

'Why don't you show the best pieces in your dining-room?' asked Dame Beatrice. 'Surely that would be a suitable setting?'

'Oh, no, not in my view. If I had gone in for figures and vases and that sort of thing, I would have had them displayed elsewhere, but plates and dishes belong in the kitchen and nowhere else.'

'You could spread the extra pieces out on this table, couldn't you?' asked Conradda. 'It would take a dozen large plates or dishes at least.'

'People might handle them. I wouldn't want that. They are hardly likely to reach up and take a dish off the dresser shelves, but it's asking too much of human nature not to pick up a plate which is lying out on a table and take a look at it. You simply cannot keep people's fingers off things if it's possible to handle them.'

'So you will not take your dishes down for us?'

'Oh, I had intended to do that. Vittorio, the step-ladder.'

He mounted it when it was brought in from the adjoining scullery and took down in turn three dishes from the top shelf.

'Leeds creamware, about . . .' he turned the first one over.

'1780,' said Vittorio. 'The strange bird in black overglaze is quite typical of the period. A good piece, not especially notable. Now this I like better, perhaps because it is of earlier date.' He handed the second dish to Dame Beatrice.

'1760, or thereabouts,' said Honfleur, 'Derby Heart-Shaped. No other factory used this particular underglaze of blue. Chinese *motifs,* as you see – a pagoda, some rather strange trees, a spray of flowers and, of course, a fenced bridge.'

'Reminiscent of the willow-pattern china of my childhood,' said Dame Beatrice, handing back the dish.

'The third dish,' said Vittorio, 'I find very pleasing. Worcester, as you see, and dating between 1770 and five years later. Very rich style of painting round the border in dark blue and gold, the scene in the middle done by somebody else, probably by Jefferyes Hamett O'Neale. Almost as good as a signature is this style of his. A charming scene, do you not think? Observe the house with its twin towers, the lake, the heavy trees, the hills in the background and the suggestion of a rocky island where the central painting meets the fruit and birds at the bottom of the border. Nice, wouldn't you say?'

Next the visitors were shown the plates which occupied the two lower shelves. Once or twice Conradda, as though instinctively, stretched out a hand to take one of the plates either from Honfleur or from Vittorio, but each time neither man appeared to be conscious of the appealing gesture; both handed the piece to Dame Beatrice.

When all the plates had been admired and descriptions and details of them provided, Conradda said:

'And now what about the pieces you say you have not room to display? The dresser is nice and I am curious to know what is hidden away in those cupboards and drawers.'

The Welsh dresser was well furnished with the receptacles she mentioned. There were three deep drawers side by side below the succession of small ones which formed the bottom shelf, and below the middle one of the three deep drawers were three more, the lowest of which, except for the skirting planks, reached the floor. On either side of these middle drawers were cupboards of considerable size.

'Oh, there's nothing more to see,' said Honfleur, 'except the less important china and the cutlery I keep for everyday use.' He pulled open the drawers and the cupboard doors and proved the truth of his words. Conradda turned to other items of interest. On one of the walls was a fine collection of carved wooden love-spoons, the traditional gifts which young Welshmen in former times had presented to young women whom they expected to marry.

Dame Beatrice had seen modern replicas of such spoons, much less intricately fashioned, which were sold to tourists, but those on Honfleur's wall were museum pieces, delightful things which must have occupied hours of patient and loving work.

She showed so much interest in them that Honfleur took each one down so that she could examine it more minutely. Conradda became restless and went apart to talk to Vittorio, who also showed no interest in the spoons.

'1856,' he said. 'Well, around that time. Of nothing but local interest, I think. What of your friend's two chargers? I see she has placed them on the table. Are they for sale, do you know?'

'I could not say. You might make an offer, I suppose.'

Vittorio approached the other two with the intention of doing this. Honfleur turned round to him and said,

'Put Dame Beatrice's chargers on the dresser, so that they show to the best advantage.'

Vittorio moved two of the pieces and then, with an eye to colour and size, placed the delftware in what seemed to him a pleasing position on the shelves. Conradda expressed her approval.

'Very nice,' she said.

'Is that where you would have placed them?' asked Vittorio, surveying his arrangement by standing further back with his head on one side. 'I think I like them like that. Now we get to business, perhaps, if Dame Beatrice is willing to part with the chargers.'

'She has already agreed to part with them,' said Honfleur.

'But there has been no talk!' said Conradda, scandalised.

'Plenty of talk,' said Dame Beatrice. 'Mr Honfleur is going to take the platters in exchange for the love-spoons.'

'Well!' exclaimed the experts with, as it seemed, one voice. Dame Beatrice cackled and Honfleur laughed.

'Oh, well,' said Conradda philosophically, 'it was a very nice dinner. A lot to drink, too.' With this naive observation she went upstairs.

'And,' said Vittorio, 'I did not collect those wooden spoons for him, so it is not the spoons I regret, but only the loss of a little business and a little fun. What does it mean, in English sport, to be given the wooden spoon?'

'This, as it happens, was Welsh sport,' said Dame Beatrice. 'These particular spoons are love-spoons.'

'Love? Ah, we understand it well, we Italians. I kiss my hand to these spoons.' He did so.

'To be handed the wooden spoon is an English metaphor signifying that one or one's team has come last in a sporting contest,' explained Honfleur.

'Like this cricket, which I do not pretend to follow?'

'What with bouncers, body-line and one-day, limited-over games, they've ruined cricket,' stated Honfleur. 'At one time it was a gentleman's pastime, but nowadays you injure the batsman or frighten him to death. Soon there won't be stroke-play any more. It will be a case of the long handle and he who ducks quickest lasts longest. Look at this knock-out tournament of sixty overs an innings! Disgraceful! A travesty of a once glorious and classic game.'

'If you are right, knock-out appears to be an appropriate word,' said Dame Beatrice. Vittorio shook his head.

'I do not understand this cricket,' he said. Dame Beatrice, summing him up, decided that he understood it in neither the literal nor the figurative sense. Honfleur began tedious explanation of what he called 'the finer points of the game' and this was interrupted by the reappearance of Conradda from upstairs.

'Well, it is getting late,' said Dame Beatrice, glancing at her wristwatch, 'and I have a forty-mile drive.'

'I came by train,' said Conradda, 'but I have booked in at a hotel for the night.'

'Which one? Perhaps I could drive you there,' said Vittorio. 'I have my car here.'

'The Parkway, a private hotel in Parks Road.'

'Then you permit me?' said Vittorio. 'I have to go along Parks Road to reach my lodging.'

Honfleur bade his guests goodnight, Dame Beatrice, who had given her chauffeur a rough estimate of the time she would be leaving, got into her own car and was taken back to the Stone House just outside the Hampshire village of Wandles Parva and Conradda and Vittorio went off together. They seemed to have formed an alliance.

On the following morning Dame Beatrice received a telephone call while she was finishing her breakfast.

'It's from Conradda Mendel,' said Laura, who had risen from table to take the call. 'She sounds urgent and *agitato*.'

'That man Vittorio,' said Conradda, when Dame Beatrice went to the telephone, 'was asking me last night whether you are interested in Chinese art. I am cautious, as you know, so I asked him what kind of Chinese art. He says mostly ceramics, although there are carpets and some jade. I stalled, of course, until I found out what he had in his mind. So he asked me if I would like to see what he has. He thought Mr Honfleur might like it, but Mr Honfleur does not like the price. This Italian says he thinks you might be a better bet. Well, I go with him to his digs and he pours me a drink and I say I cannot stay long because my hotel closes at midnight and I do not want to knock people up, so while we are having this drink he says he will show me one or two things which may be of interest and if I get you to buy he will let me have something on the cheap, a really nice price, for my shop.'

'Is that sort of offer usual?'

'Not unusual, if a favour is being done. Well, I made no promises, of course, but I said I would like to see what he had to show me, but not carpets. He showed me the collection of jade first. Jade is nice, but there was nothing of any great interest and I did not betray any enthusiasm. I think this made him a little bit desperate. He said, "Well, I have some nice pots."

Conradda paused as though to allow Dame Beatrice to comment, but all she heard from the other end was:

'Oh, yes?'

'Do you think anybody can tap this line?'

'I have no idea.'

'Are you alone?'

'Yes, quite alone. The servants are in the kitchen and Laura is in the dining-room finishing her breakfast.'

'Good. I shall speak quietly, like this. Are you able to hear?'

'Perfectly. You are making my flesh creep.'

'So mine when I saw what was shown me. You know that I have made a special study of ceramics?'

'I noticed that you were careful not to say so when we were at Basil Honfleur's house.'

'It does not do to say too much. Dame Beatrice, I was shown such articles as nobody unknown to the trade could have come by honestly. There was T'ang, there was *Famille Rose* of Ch'ien Lung period, there was enamelled porcelain of Chia Ching period, *Famille Verte* of K'ang Hsi period, painted stoneware of Sung dynasty. I have seen nothing like it outside a museum or perhaps the very best of private collections. It is fabulous.'

'Why could it not have been come by honestly?'

'Because I have seen descriptions very like some of these pieces before. You know where? In the lists the police issue to people in my line of business. Of course I shall not split on him because I do not want to cause trouble. Also I have not time to spare in police courts.'

'But, my dear Miss Mendel, if you are sure these things are stolen, you might be in trouble yourself if you do not report your findings.'

'I shall say nothing. I do not wish to get my throat cut. That Vittorio is an assassin. All I say to you is this: however nice a price he asks you, *do not buy.*'

CHAPTER 2

The Missing Coach-Drivers

Almost a year went by before Dame Beatrice saw Basil Honfleur again, and when she did the meeting was neither of his seeking nor of hers, although both consented to its taking place.

As for the Jewish antique-dealer, she had telephoned again just after Christmas to say that she had sold both her shops and was going to America.

'I suppose when she knew she'd been shown some pretty hot goods,' said Laura, 'she was in a bit of a flap, especially as she didn't intend to go to the police.

'You don't think she bought the stuff from Vittorio at a reasonable figure and took it to America with her?'

'Your imagination, as usual, is running away with you. If *she* recognised some of the pieces, possibly others would be able to do so. I hardly think it would be worth the risk. The receivers of stolen goods, knowing them to have been stolen, face heavy penalties if they are found out, you know, and Miss Mendel is not a foolish or a reckless woman.'

'Would it be easy to take the contents of high-class antique shops out of the country?'

'I do not think she has attempted to do that. I gather that she sold all her business interests over here before she left, and that, I imagine, would include the stock. But to matters of greater moment: what did you make of the letter from the chairman of

County Motors which came by this morning's post?'

'A cry from the heart. Honfleur's bosses, aren't they? Are you dipping into the affair? They certainly want your help.'

'I had better go and see them and find out more about the matter. It sounds interesting.'

'Do I accompany you?'

'No, George will take me. When the interview is over I shall come straight back here unless there is any good reason for my remaining, but I really cannot imagine what the motor-coach company thinks I can do in an affair of this sort. It is a case for the police.'

As a result of a telephone call to the chairman, who had written from his private address, Dame Beatrice found herself once again confronting Basil Honfleur, this time in his office from which he worked out the schedules and appointed the drivers for his branch of County Motors. It was what might be called the mother house of the coach company and his job was a good one. He had to report at board meetings, but otherwise he was his own master and enjoyed almost unlimited freedom, except from responsibility.

He greeted Dame Beatrice cordially and said that he was glad to see her.

'It's these missing drivers of ours,' he went on, when they were seated. 'A most mysterious business. We can't think what can have happened to them.'

'No, indeed,' Dame Beatrice agreed. 'All the same, if I may invoke the formidable shade of Lady Bracknell and reiterate her concise opinion on such matters, to lose one driver may be a misfortune; to lose two looks like carelessness. I suppose your directors have informed the police?'

'Yes, of course, but you know what the police are! Report a missing child and they'll turn on the whole works — dog-handlers, walkie-talkies, make life hell for every male in the neighbourhood, drag every river, canal, gravel-pit and dirty pond in the area and set a whole squad of flatties to search woods and beat bushes. Report a missing man, particularly if he's married and the father of a family, and what do they do? Look at you as though you need to have your head examined and ask whether you know how many men go missing from their homes every year and are never traced.'

'A fair enough question, of course. There comes a time in most men's lives when they sicken of the trivial round, the common task, and yearn to explore fresh woods and pastures new.'

'The police seem to think these men don't *want* to be found.'

'The police may well be right. They so often *are* right in matters which fall within their vast experience.'

'You mean you're not interested? The directors did hope you might be. They say they could believe that *one* of our steady, respectable fellows had felt the urge to cut loose and go missing, but that I must surely admit that for two of them to go off within the space of four weeks, and apparently vanish without trace, does take a bit of swallowing. They say even the police admit that and so, I suppose, do I.'

'Oh, I admit it, too, but there is an aspect of the matter which no doubt the police have touched on.'

'How do you mean?'

'Well, it seems to me that your drivers are in almost a unique position, even more so than sailors or commercial travellers. There they are, under no official supervision once the tour leaves the depôt. They have a suitcase already packed, money in their pockets and anything from five days to a fortnight, I suppose, in which to put their plans into operation.'

'I think that's an exaggerated view of the amount of freedom they have. Hotel managers, for example, would soon be on the blower to us if a coach failed to arrive on the appointed day.'

'Ah, yes, of course. To turn to another aspect, I suppose your men are happy in their work?'

'Happy? I don't see why they shouldn't be. We're a subsidiary of the bus company, you know, and we recruit our men from among their drivers. It's a promotion for those whom we employ. The pay is better and the conditions are excellent. Then, of course, there are the perks.'

'The perks?'

'The drivers put up at the same hotels as the passengers and get the same food. At the end of each tour most of the passengers put something into the hat and when you consider. that we run the tours from the end of April to the middle of October, these tips can amount to something pretty substantial. It's not a job that chaps would chuck up without a jolly good reason, I can tell you.'

'I see. No wonder the defection of two of these fortunate men has upset and perplexed the directors. I should be interested to hear more. Begin at the beginning, if you will. I am intrigued by what you tell me. How does it all start? What happens after the middle of October, I mean?'

'In November we issue a leaflet setting out what we expect to do during the following year. About mid-December we follow this up with a glossy, colourful brochure with photographs, little route-maps, full details of all tours, prices, insurance cover, hotels, luncheon stops, special attractions and so on. These brochures can be picked up at any of our booking offices and we also send one to every passenger who has ever travelled with us over the last five years or so.'

'Really? You have a regular clientèle, then?'

'Oh, rather! People travel with us year after year. Some of them book again – provisionally, of course – almost as soon as they get back. There's terrific competition for the front seats, as you'd expect. Of course, we have a great deal to offer. If they did the tours privately, using the same lunch-stops and hotels as we do, it could cost them twice as much as they pay us. On our very popular nine-day tours, for example, which go out on the Saturday morning and return in the evening of the Sunday week, we reckon to put the coach up at two four-star hotels and the other hotels are usually three-star or, out in the wilds, the very best we can get.'

'So you receive no complaints from your passengers.'

Basil Honfleur laughed.

'Of course we get complaints, and we investigate every one. After all, our whole concern rests upon good-will and satisfaction. Sometimes the same complaint comes from several sources. In that case, as often as not, we remove that particular hotel from our list. Usually we find, though, that solitary individual complaints are not justified. There are people who make a hobby of complaining. Most of them write to the newspapers or the BBC, some write to their MP and some write to us. They don't seem happy unless they're nursing some fancied grievance. However, they are the exceptions so far as our passengers are concerned and as they usually travel with us only the once, we're not too terribly concerned with them. Of course, as I said, we do investigate every complaint we receive, just in case there's something in it, but there very seldom is.'

'And what kind of people travel with you more than once?'

'Our passengers are mostly middle-aged and elderly, and there's a preponderance of women – lonely spinsters, you know, or a couple of widows travelling together for company. We get more married couples than we used to, though. It means that Dad can have a chance to admire the scenery and take his ease on holiday, instead of being tied to the driver's seat of the family car and having to keep his eyes on the road.'

'Yes, I can appreciate that.'

'At one time the people who booked with us liked travelling but had no car. That is far from being the case today. Years ago, too, the kind who took coach tours had never previously been inside a hotel. That certainly is not true today. You hear them discussing holidays in Greece and Yugoslavia, not to mention Italy and the Costa Brava. They're not poor, our present-day clients. You should see what they buy in the way of souvenirs and presents. How the devil they get all the stuff home I sometimes wonder. You find, too, that a number of them have already had a holiday on the Continent that very same summer.

They tell us they like to take one of our tours 'to unwind'. Times have changed with a vengeance! Instead of saving up for a rainy day they reckon the Welfare State will provide the umbrella for that, so the slogan is: *You can't take it with you.* And, of course, their children are in good jobs, so they don't need any future provision made for them. Add the bogeyman Inflation, and you can't blame them for their attitude. I wonder, though, how much longer it can last.'

'However, while it does last, your company is not ungrateful.'

'Well, hang it all, our passengers get their money's worth, and they know it. Of course, they'd do things a lot cheaper in a caravan or at a holiday camp, but they prefer to travel in our coaches. After all, it's a grand way to see the country, even if you can't choose your stopping-places. Then, something which appeals very much to the women, all the meals are laid on and there's no washing up to do.'

'The meals? Ah, yes, a most important part of any holiday.'

'Also, there are no problems for them with regard to their luggage. Once it's on the coach we handle it for them everywhere they stay. Apart from putting it outside their bedroom doors so that we can collect it while they're at breakfast each morning, they don't have to tote it about at all, and that's a big concession to elderly people.'

'And the meals?'

'Oh, we get very few complaints about those. We used also to provide early tea and daily and Sunday newspapers free of charge, but most hotels haven't the staff nowadays to take round early tea, so they put a contraption in each room so that people can make their own. We discontinued newspapers because of the cost, and the same goes for afternoon teas.'

'No afternoon teas? That must have caused some heart-burning.'

'Oh, the driver always pulls up at some suitable place at some time between four o'clock and five, so that those who can't do without their cuppa can get one. The only difference is that it isn't included nowadays in the fare. We do include after-lunch and after-dinner coffee, though. We always ask to have it served in the lounge. It makes a social occasion of it, you see, with general conversation. Helps people to get together and sort themselves out.'

'And do people object to paying extra for their teas? Would they be inclined to reproach the driver?'

'I've never heard of that. From our point of view, you know, the teas were a waste of money, particularly in Scotland and the West Country. When people have eaten bread, butter and jam, baps, scones and cakes, or Cornish pasties and perhaps stewed fruit and clotted cream at tea-time, many of them are not hungry enough to do justice to a three-or four-course dinner, especially when they've had a cooked breakfast and a three-course lunch as well as their tea.'

'How are the halts for tea-time organised?'

'They're not. It's up to the drivers to pick out suitable stopping-places.'

'That seems to lay an unreasonable burden on them, does it not?'

'Well, I admit they don't like it much. The easiest stops nowadays are on the motorways, of course, but we don't use those more than we can help because it means such monotonous travel. In remote districts, though, it's sometimes very difficult to find a suitable café at about the right time of day, and then perhaps the driver does come in for some criticism.'

'Would that be sufficient to cause disaffection among your drivers?'

'Enough to make them pack in the job and beetle off without giving notice, do you mean? Oh, I shouldn't think they'd do that. After all, if they don't like the conditions, they have only to say so and go back to the buses. There would be no need to disappear off the face of the earth as these two fellows seem to have done.'

'It really does seem curious, but how do *I* come into the affair?'

'Well, the board of directors seem to think they'd like you to make your own enquiries without reference to what the police may or may not intend to do.'

'Their resources are very much greater than mine, you know.'

'I pointed that out and said I didn't see what you could do.'

'Would you asperse me and my efforts?'

'No, of course not. As my chairman pointed out, the police are not really interested, so their enquiries will be a matter of routine, not of urgency.'

'Have you yourself formed any theory which might account for your men's disappearance?'

'Not unless they've both had domestic troubles. We've contacted passengers and so have the police, but there isn't a clue. Nothing has gone wrong on any of our tours, so far as we know. These two drivers simply disappeared and haven't been seen since. I cannot understand it. I'll tell you something, though, which convinces my chairman that there's some kind of mystery afoot. In Pembrokeshire we mislaid a coach as well as its driver. It reappeared, but miles from where the driver should have left it. We found it abandoned in Swansea.'

'And where, exactly, did you mislay it?'

'It disappeared at some time during the middle of the morning from Dantwylch, right out on the west coast. That's miles away from Swansea, where the Welsh police tracked it down.'

'This, I gather, was the second incident, but you have mislaid no other coaches?'

'No. We're glad of that, of course, but it's the missing drivers who concern us. The driver-courier is the king-pin of any tour. He's the all-pervasive, all-persuasive adhesive which binds the coach-party together and holds it firm. He's the father-figure, if you like, of the tourists. They trust him absolutely.'

'And you have lost a couple of these paternal fixatives! Dear me!'

'And replacements aren't easy to find, especially as we've got another chap on sick leave. We're having to over-schedule our other men, and that's not going to make us very popular with them. A driver isn't a bit thrilled when he comes back from six days in Yorkshire on Friday night and is told he's got to take another coach-load for a nine-day trip to Scotland starting early on Saturday morning.'

'I sympathise with him.'

'So do I, but what can I do? We keep within the legal limits of working hours, of course, even when we have to pile it on like that, and we try to even out the extra duties so far as we possibly can, but it's very unfair to switch a man on to a route he has never travelled before. He doesn't know the hotels or where to stop for mid-morning coffee or afternoon tea, let alone give out bits of history and other information which the passengers expect. Of course we pay out bonuses, but it isn't, any of it, good enough and it can't go on.'

'Have you spoken to your other drivers about the disappearances? Has none of them anything to suggest?'

'Nothing at all. They've heard no rumours; they've been told no secrets. They assure us that the missing men had given no indication whatever that anything was wrong. If there *had* been anything amiss, I'm sure they would have known. They're a pretty close-knit bunch and have been together for years. The passengers get pretty close-knit, too. It's very interesting to see how sociable and gregarious most people are.'

'You mean many of them have travelled together before?'

'No, not that. It's unlikely that they would, because, although they travel with us time and again, naturally they choose different tours each year. All the same, it's true to say that whereas a collection of individuals boards the coach at the starting place and the pick-up points, all of them keeping a jealous eye on their rights and their possessions, by the time the second day comes round they're a unit; they've fused; they're an entity. But you *must* have the proper chap in charge for it to work that way.'

'You lost one man and had a coach borrowed and then abandoned in Wales and you lost another man in the Peak District, you tell me. It seems that there must surely be some connection.'

'By the way, the Derbyshire man, Noone, was the first, not the second, to disappear.'

'I wonder whether that fact has any significance? Derbyshire and West Wales, where, as you say, the disappearances took place, are a good many miles apart. According to the letter I received from your chairman, however, there does seem to have been one connection between the two incidents.'

'Oh? What was that? Something significant, do you mean?'

'I hardly know whether it is significant or not, but it is certainly interesting because it seems to have provided a requisite opportunity for the drivers to vanish if they had planned to do so.'

'That's interesting. How do you mean?'

'Your chairman informs me that in each case the coach was empty when the driver disappeared. Could this mean that the passengers were out of the coach long enough for something to happen to the driver?'

'Yes, could be. The Derbyshire tour includes an afternoon visit to Hulliwell Hall and we always allow plenty of time for that. There is a free morning and then the coach sets off immediately after lunch and the passengers can take their time over their sightseeing. Those who want tea can buy it at the Hall and the coach gets back to the hotel in time for people to take a bath and to change for dinner.'

'Whereabouts is the hotel?'

'We generally use a hotel in Buxton, but for this one particular tour we did not.'

'Any special reason?'

'Yes, as a matter of fact, there was. They had a vast literary conference in Buxton that week and the hotels were full, so we had to make other arrangements.'

'At short notice?'

'Oh, no. Buxton told us in March.'

'So where did the coach stay?'

'We fixed up a place in Dovedale, but I can't see that the change of hotel would account for the disappearance of the driver.'

'Does the coach remain at the same hotel for the duration of the tour? Are there, I mean, daily outings, or does the coach move on to other hotels?'

'It varies. Mostly the coach moves on, but the Derbyshire tour stays all five nights in the same place and goes out each day as you suggest. In the case of the Welsh tour, we stay a night in Monmouth, three nights at Tenby, a night at Towyn and the last night in Hereford.'

Dame Beatrice's next interview, by mutual arrangement, was with the chairman of County Motors. She made further enquiry about the coach tours.

'West Wales?' he said. 'Well, we think it's a particularly good tour, very popular, and Daigh, the missing driver, was one of our best men.'

'Well, we must try to find him. What other tours are there?'

'Oh, you *are* going to take on the job, then? My board will be delighted. Another tour goes up to Scotland, staying one night in Yorkshire, one in Edinburgh and two in a new hotel near Fort William, from which we go over to Skye for a day. We have many others, but the Skye tour is one of the most popular. We come back through Pitlochry and Perth, go on to Edinburgh and then across the Lowlands to Carlisle and the Lakes, and so home by way of Grange-over-Sands and Warwick.'

'And when, exactly, did the drivers disappear?'

'Noone vanished while his passengers were visiting Hulliwell Hall. They had the morning free to explore Dovedale or go to Buxton and then the coach moved off at two o'clock to give them plenty of time to see the Hall and have tea there, if they wanted it. Honfleur says they would be out of the coach for the better part of a couple of hours.'

'And during that time the driver vanished and has not been

traced. But the coach, I assume, was where he had left it?'

'Near enough, although we think it had been moved. Anyway, after the passengers had hung about and made all sorts of enquiries, one of them — most improperly, of course — drove the coach back to the hotel. He then made a report which, when the driver did not show up that evening, the management relayed to us.'

'And your second man?'

'Daigh got himself *and* his coach spirited away during a long coffee-stop in Dantwylch. This was on a trip out from Tenby to visit Dantwylch Cathedral and the ruins of the bishop's palace.'

'A *long* coffee-stop? How long?'

'About an hour and a half. The coach pulled up at a spot convenient to the sight-seers and then went off to the local car-park. The arrangement was that it would return for the passengers at a given time to take them on to Fishguard for lunch, but, of course, it never arrived.'

'So what happened then?'

'Some of the passengers went to the car park and found that the coach had been there, but had only stayed a very short time. They returned to the others and they all hung about until a policeman told them they were obstructing the footway. They informed him of what had happened. The upshot was that a local coach was laid on and the day's outing proceeded according to plan, except that the passengers arrived extremely late for lunch. Eventually the coach was traced to Swansea. We sent up another driver as soon as we got a 'phone call from the manager of the hotel at Tenby after the passengers had been taken back there for the night, and the police soon traced our own coach, so that was all right so far, except that they haven't traced Daigh.'

'It seems a most mysterious business. Can you supply me with a list of the passengers who took these two tours and give me their addresses?'

'Yes, of course. Honfleur's desk-clerks will know. I'll call him.

They'll have all the details at his office.'

'And can I possibly find out which of the passengers have travelled with you before? I understand from Mr Honfleur that the majority of your clients, having sampled the amenities you offer, are inclined very much to book with you again.'

'Again *and* again, most of them. It's very gratifying. I will certainly obtain the information you require and will let you have it at the earliest possible moment. I am so grateful that you are prepared to help us. I am not at all in agreement with Honfleur that it is a waste of your time. The police will do their best, but I think a private enquiry may obtain quicker results.'

CHAPTER 3

Hulliwell Hall

Dame Beatrice spent the whole of the following day studying the lists of names and addresses she had been given so that she could make her choice of witnesses. She was working entirely in the dark, for Basil Honfleur could give her no further information. He had met none of the passengers. There were thirty names on the Derbyshire list and twenty-eight people had taken the Welsh tour.

The ideal procedure, she supposed, would have been to interview each and e very passenger, as the police had done, but she felt that time was important, so for the Derbyshire witness she chose Vernon Tedworthy. He had a telephone number, which expedited matters, so she called him up and asked whether she might visit him.

Vernon Tedworthy was a retired schoolmaster. A pencilled note on the Derbyshire list informed Dame Beatrice that his only previous experience of touring with County Motors had been in 1971, when he had travelled with his wife on a trip to Yorkshire.

When he and Dame Beatrice met, he told her that he had intended to stay at his school (where he was deputy headmaster) until his sixty-fifth birthday, but two things had caused him to change his mind and retire at the optional age of sixty years. One was the death of his wife when he was fifty-nine; the other was that his school, a good, well-run, trouble-free Secondary Modern establishment of three hundred and fifty boys, each of them known by name to the headmaster and his staff of ten picked and dedicated men, was to be turned into a two-thousand strong, mixed Comprehensive.

It was much less than certain that Vernon Tedworthy's headmaster would be offered the captaincy of this gargantuan hydra, and even less certain that Tedworthy would retain his post as deputy head. That would go to some young man with a university degree to flourish, a young man who, as like as not, would do little classroom teaching, but who would be employed mostly in an administrative capacity only, with plenty of paper-work to fill up his time, but with little or no contact with the real life of the school as personified by its couple of thousand boys and girls.

'Not for me,' said Tedworthy. He had given in his notice of retirement to take effect at the end of the Easter term following his sixtieth birthday. 'Why on earth they want to muck up perfectly good schools, whether they're Sec. Mod. or grammar schools, to satisfy the sacred cow of Equality of Opportunity, I don't know. I know it *sounds* all right, but some animals will always be more equal than others, don't you think?'

After his retirement he had sold his house and lived for a time with his daughter and her husband and family, but in the following spring he had bought a small bungalow in Dorset and lived alone there except for occasional visits from relatives and friends. He ran a small car, but when it came to holidays he decided that he would try another coach tour. It was not good to lead too solitary a life.

He remembered that on their previous trip he and his wife had enjoyed themselves and had made many temporary friends – temporary in the sense that, although addresses had been exchanged and promises made of keeping in touch, nothing had come of what had been merely an expression of holiday enthusiasm and euphoria.

He picked up a brochure at his local coach station and decided upon a tour of the Peak District. It was a part of the country which he had not visited and which had no associations with his wife. He thought, too, that six days would be enough to show him whether it was the kind of holiday he could still enjoy, or whether perhaps a fishing holiday of a solitary kind would be preferable in the future.

There were only five people at the start of the tour; a few others were picked up along the route and the main body joined the coach at Canonbury. Up to that point he had had the seat to himself, but he realised that this was not likely to last, and it did not.

Before the coach moved off from the Canonbury bus station, the driver, his tally complete, introduced himself to his passengers.

'I am Cyril Noone, your driver-courier. Good morning, ladies and gentlemen. I hope you will all have a pleasant tour and we'll hope for the best from the weather. You have had your coffee break for this morning, so our next stop is for lunch in Cheltenham. As we go along I shall be indicating any items of interest we pass on the road and I shall also be telling you how long we have for lunch and tea and so forth, and what the arrangements are for our hotel and the time we start off for our first trip tomorrow morning. I don't need to tell you that good time-keeping is essential on these tours, so I am sure you will all get back to the coach punctually, so that we don't have to rush things. Thank you.'

At Canonbury Tedworthy's partner had joined him. She was odd-one-out in a threesome which consisted of husband, wife and wife's sister, all of advanced middle age but not elderly. He hoped that Miss Eildon (her name on the passenger list with which he had been supplied) would not prove talkative. Courteously he offered her the window seat which he had booked for himself, but she thanked him, refused it and said that she preferred to talk across the gangway to her relatives.

'That's if I want to talk,' she said. 'I think to look at the scenery is better, don't you?' Thankfully Tedworthy agreed. At the first lunch stop he included himself as the fourth member of her party at a table for four and this convenient and agreeable arrangement continued for the rest of the tour.

The coach-load proved to be a mild and orderly party and soon split up into recognisable groups, any lone souls being absorbed in kindly fashion so that nobody was obviously segregated. Tedworthy was well pleased with all the arrangements. He liked the company he was keeping, the hotel where they were to stay for five nights was well situated and comfortable and the meals were good.

The first morning in Dovedale was wet, but newspapers were available, although not included in the price of the tour. Most of the men settled in the lounge to read while the women formed groups and gossiped. When the bar opened at eleven there was an exodus and lunch was served at twelve-thirty because there was a coach-trip to Matlock Bath in the afternoon.

Breakfast was at eight on the following morning. The rain had cleared away and the party, leaving the hotel at a quarter past nine, spent an enjoyable day. There was a halt at Tissington to see one of the florally decorated wells (no longer restricted only to Ascension Day) and another short stop at Eyam. The last was unscheduled, but Tedworthy was anxious to take a photograph of the Saxon cross in the churchyard, a matter of more interest to him than was Cyril Noone's account of the Reverend William Mompesson and his heroic villagers who, at the time of the Great Plague, remained in their village and died there instead of fleeing for safety and risking a spread of infection.

The next day was the one which nobody on the coach was ever likely to forget, for it was the day on which Cyril Noone disappeared. The morning arrangements included a trip to Buxton, but Tedworthy opted for a lonely walk in the Dove valley beside the water. He saw the rest of the party off at nine o'clock, then picked up his ashplant and set out. Lunch was to be early, so he looked at his watch, divided his time and decided to allow himself a quarter of an hour for a pint before the meal was served.

The day was fine and sunny after the rain. He had made up his mind not to hurry, for he thought that a man who hastens his steps alongside Izaak Walton's stream is worse than a fool.

It was easy walking. The lower slopes of the hills were thickly wooded and the trees were still heavy with summer foliage, but above them was the stark grimness of the limestone, culminating in the dominating, pointed summit of Thorpe Cloud.

He passed limestone holes in the cliff, some large enough to be called caverns, crossed a narrow wooden bridge and came, in a very shallow reach of water which rippled and reflected the blue of the sky, to stepping stones. The path curved with the river. A kingfisher flashed past and a dipper, a surprising bird to find in the Derbyshire dales, was perched on a large stone with its legs in the water, bobbing and bowing in search of aquatic food.

With no premonition of what was to come, Tedworthy spent a delightful morning and when he got back to the hotel in time for his pint of beer he spotted the coachdriver in the lounge, so he picked up his tankard at the bar and joined Noone at a window which overlooked the hills.

'Pleasant walk, Mr Tedworthy?'

'Very. Can't beat this part of the world. Will you join me?'

'Very kind of you, but I don't touch anything midday when I've got a trip in the afternoon. Did you get a good picture in the churchyard yesterday?'

'I hope so. I'm rather keen on these old stone crosses and this one was a beauty.'

'So long as you didn't want to pinch it and have me stick it in the boot! We carry some rare peculiar things now and again, you know, but a stone cross would be a new one for me to tote along.'

The coach left at two for the afternoon excursion to Hulliwell Hall. It was one of several great houses in that part of the country and one that Tedworthy looked forward to visiting, for the building spanned six centuries and the earlier parts of it were unspoiled, since additions and repairs had been made, but the successive owners had permitted no other alterations.

The driver parked the coach as near the entrance as he was allowed to do, and this left the passengers with only a short, steep, rather rough climb to the ancient gatehouse.

As he had proved that morning, Tedworthy, who was glad enough of company at meals, preferred to be on his own when there was sightseeing to be done. He climbed the rough slope and ducked under a mediaeval archway inside the gatehouse.

Just beyond the archway was the entrance to a small, stuffy museum, so he made a cursory inspection of bits of broken pottery, leather jugs, Roman coins, Victorian dolls and a scale model of Hulliwell Hall itself and then pased on to explore the actual edifice.

To his relief, there was no question of having to join a conducted party. He inspected the kitchen, the fourteenth century chapel, the banqueting hall and the Tudor long gallery and then strolled out on to the terrace. Behind him were mullioned windows and twin towers. Below him were rose gardens, a park with noble trees and the river with its narrow bridge. It was a fine prospect and he tried to imagine himself the owner of such a place.

He descended a flight of steps from the terrace to the rose-garden and took snapshots of the house, then he decided to return to the coach and smoke a quiet cigarette. If the driver had locked the coach and gone off for a bit, well, the weather was clement, the scenery pleasant and there was not enough wind to spoil the pleasure of smoking.

The coach, however, was open, although there was no sign of Cyril Noone. This surprised Tedworthy, since most of the passengers had left coats, mackintoshes, umbrellas and hand-luggage on the racks, and had been assured by Noone that the coach was always locked and their property perfectly safe at the various stopping-places

Tedworthy, who had enjoyed everything else that day, enjoyed his cigarette. He spread himself comfortably over the seat and by the time he had finished his leisurely smoke the others had come straggling back. Some had had tea at a discreetly-sited modern pavilion at the back of the house; others had noted familiar plants in the gardens; all were impressed by the size and beauty of the house and some spoke in admiring ignorance, others with self-conscious knowledge, about the pictures in the long gallery; some speculated on the chances that the house was haunted, the consensus of female opinion being that it most certainly was.

Time passed, the coach filled up and gradually a certain impatience began to make itself felt. It was more than half an hour later than the time specified by Noone for his passengers' return to the coach. There began to be murmurings.

'He can't be at the pub,' said one of the men. 'It's out of hours.'

'Too far from here, anyway,' said another, indicating the rural surroundings. 'We left the last village miles back.'

'Can't be engine trouble,' said somebody else. 'If it was, he or a mechanic would be tinkering with it.'

'Perhaps he went into the house and got lost,' said one of the women. 'I should think it would be easy enough in a place that size.'

'Perhaps he's been taken ill,' said another voice. 'These coach-drivers always suffer with their stomachs. It's wrenching that steering-wheel round the bends that does it.'

They waited half-an-hour longer. Some got out of the coach and strolled about or climbed to the entrance to the gatehouse to look at the view.

'Wish I'd had a cup of tea while I had the chance,' said a

woman wistfully, 'but I suppose you'd have to pay again to go inside.'

'You don't want to go wandering off now, Doris,' said her husband. 'Ten to one the driver will be back any minute.'

But the minutes passed and the driver did not appear. Tedworthy, his schoolmaster sense of responsibility and leadership asserting itself, went up to the house to make enquiries. The man who issued tickets at a small hut just inside the gatehouse was certain that Noone had not passed his portals.

'I know him well,' he said. 'Spring and autumn tours, when it's quiet and I haven't got much to do, he always comes along and has a crack with me. Besides, nobody can pass into the courtyard without they buy a ticket from me. You can see that for yourself, sir. Oh, no, he hasn't come up here.'

Dissatisfied but convinced, Tedworthy returned to the coach and made his report. Another half-hour passed. Those who had left the coach returned to it. There was grumbling, a good deal of comment and speculation and a growing alarm and impatience. At last the man who had mentioned the pub came up to Tedworthy's seat.

'Look, old man,' he said, 'I used to drive a tank in the desert. How about you navigating and me taking this bus back to the hotel? We can't stick here for ever. The hotel will have the means to contact the tour people and tell 'em what's happened. What do you say? Be missing our dinner if we stay here much longer.'

Tedworthy was dubious.

'There may be a question of insurance if one of us drives the coach,' he said. 'Put it to the meeting. Let's have a majority verdict.'

The verdict was almost unanimous, so the ex-Desert Rat, guided by Tedworthy, brought the coach safely back to the inn in Dovedale.

There was discussion at the dinner table as to what would happen when Noone came back eventually to Hulliwell Hall and found the coach gone. Tedworthy assured his table that among the drivers of commercial vehicles there was a brotherhood of the road and that it would be hard lines indeed if Noone could not hitch a lift back to the hotel. There remained a spare seat at dinner, however, and an empty and clean coffee-cup in the lounge. By the time the last of the party had finished a game of bridge and retired upstairs, the missing coach-driver had not re-appeared.

In the morning there was an empty chair at the breakfast table and Tedworthy and the tank-soldier, joined by a decorative lady who was a retired hairdresser, sought another interview with the manager of the hotel, who already had been informed of the driver's absence. He told them that a coach would be sent out from Buxton for the day's outing, and that before nightfall another driver would be arriving from headquarters and would take over the tour if Noone had not put in an appearance. Meanwhile the police had been informed and a search was already under way.

The police also sought information from the passengers. Before Noone's coach and its new driver could move off, every person on it was interrogated, but the answers provided no help and no clue. Noone had been his cheerful, confident self that day. He had issued specific instructions as to the time he intended to move off from Hulliwell Hall. There had been no hitch in the arrangements until he failed to turn up and take his party back to the hotel. Nobody had anything to suggest.

The new driver turned up later that night and the rest of the tour was carried out according to the promises made in the company's brochure. Noone's disappearance was was a nine days' wonder so far as most of the passengers were concerned. Only a very few, Tedworthy included, gave the matter much more thought except as a story to tell in the pub or at the table when the tour was over.

Dame Beatrice, who had selected Tedworthy as her first guinea-pig, decided to begin her search for Driver Noone by covering the ground for herself. Tedworthy had made a first-class witness. He had been lucid, unbiased and exact. He also knew just how long a time had elapsed between his leaving the coach for Hulliwell Hall and his return to it to smoke his cigarette.

'I wanted to make sure I'd meet the driver's deadline,' he said. 'I've had too much experience of rounding-up kids on school outings to be a culprit myself.'

'So you spent an hour and ten minutes in the Hall, and an hour and a half had been allowed. Was the coach in the same place, when you returned to it?'

'Near enough.'

'Near enough?'

'It was about thirty yards further from the path we had to take to walk up to the house.'

'How do you know? I mean, how can you be sure?'

'Where we got out of the coach there was a chunk of rock — limestone, I think — at the side of the road. I noticed it, although I'm not much of a geologist; I do photography in my spare time. I noticed it again when I passed it on my way back to the coach. The boulder wouldn't have moved, so the coach must have done.'

'Did you wonder why the coach had been moved?'

'No, not to say wonder. There were a number of visitors, apart from our lot, so J supposed our driver had moved the coach to accommodate somebody's car.'

'And was there a car opposite the boulder you noticed?'

'No, but a car could have been driven away again, of course, before I got back.'

'It did not occur to you that your coach might have made quite a journey while your party was going over the Hall?'

'No, I never thought of that, but I suppose it could have done. It was a long time for the driver to hang about.'

'When you got back to the coach, you say it was open. Was it merely unlocked or was the door set back?'

'Oh, the door was wide open. It is operated from the driver's seat, you know, and I had noticed that when Noone got in after a stop he did so by unlocking the emergency door at the side of the coach near the back and then coming forward to his seat to let us in at the front. I assumed this was the only way of opening up the coach once the passengers' door was properly closed. Mind you, I thought it was damned careless of him to have left the coach wide open with nobody in it, considering that people had left all sorts of gear on their seats and on the rack.'

'What did you think had happened to him?'

'At the time I thought he'd merely strolled off to speak to other coach-drivers and pass the time of day. We were by no means the only coach-party there.'

'You did not think he had moved off in the coach and that perhaps somebody else had brought it back and had not parked it in exactly the same spot?'

'No, that never occurred to me; and he wouldn't have driven off to get the tank topped up, because he told us he'd taken on fourteen gallons before we started out after lunch.'

The police, it turned out, had already explored that particular avenue. The only garage the coach had visited that day was the one nearest to the hotel in Dovedale. Here the fourteen gallons had been taken on board and the drive to Hulliwell Hall had been a short one and could not have used up any considerable amount of fuel.

Dame Beatrice put up at the hotel which the coach-party had used and then she visited Hulliwell Hall. She pulled up opposite the boulder which Tedworthy had noticed, left her chauffeur in charge of the car and took the rough path up to the great house.

The original structure, in effect, had been a castle dating from the late twelfth century. On to it had been grafted a large parlour and a chapel, both of the fourteenth century, and a magnificent long gallery of Elizabethan date. Another parlour had been added at the same time, and was known as the dining-parlour. It was wainscoted, had a large window decorated with coats of arms, a very fine fireplace and a painted ceiling.

The banqueting hall was larger and a couple of centuries earlier in date. It retained its minstrels' gallery and the dais and long tables of its mediaeval period, but there was modern clear glass in the window which was furnished with two stone corner seats approached by a steep stone step.

Dame Beatrice allowed herself the hour and ten minutes which Tedworthy had given as the time he himself had spent at the Hall and then she returned to her car. Of one thing she had made certain. She had looked out of every window in the rooms open to visitors. From none of them had her car been visible. She had allowed for the superior height of a motor-coach, but had calculated that it also would be out of sight from the windows. Not even the most observant visitor to the Hall, therefore, could have said whether Noone's coach had been driven away, and, if so, when it had returned and how long it had been absent.

'I have discovered little that was not already known to the police,' said Dame Beatrice, when she met Honfleur again. 'There was an interval of roughly an hour and a quarter between the time the passengers left the coach to visit Hulliwell Hall and the time when the first of them returned to it.

'From evidence given to me by Mr Tedworthy, a most sensible and observant witness, it is pretty certain that the coach had been moved while it was vacant except for the driver. I attempted to check where it went by enquiring at the nearest public house, but obtained no definite information, as coach-drivers, you may be relieved to know, do not indulge in alcoholic refreshment in the middle of the day.

'On the way to the public house my car had passed a church and I noticed that the sexton and an assistant were engaged in digging a grave. I stopped the car and went into the churchyard to make enquiries, but it seems that the person to be buried was a woman who died a natural death and who had lived in the village all her life.

'Mr Tedworthy asserts that, when he returned to the coach, it was open, in spite of the fact that the passengers had left possessions on the seats and the racks. This further inclines me to the belief that the coach had been moved some distance and that when it returned, not exactly to the same spot as before, your driver was no longer with it. I informed the local police of my opinion and they agree with me that the coach might have been moved, but not necessarily very far. They say that their search for Driver Noone is being prosecuted with the utmost endeavour, but I am inclined to think that they still believe his disappearance was voluntary.'

'I suppose we must consider it as a possibility,' said Basil Honfleur. 'Well, what's the next move?'

'I think we must leave Derbyshire to the police for the time being and I will see what Dantwylch has to offer. If one thing is clear, it is that your two drivers are either part of a conspiracy . . .'

'I reject that theory entirely!'

'. . . or that they are the victims of one.'

'But why?'

'One keeps an open mind. The key to the matter, of course, is the coach which disappeared from Dantwylch and so mysteriously reappeared in Swansea. Why Swansea?'

'I don't know, except that, since the troubles escalated in Northern Ireland, we have altered one of our schedules.'

'Oh, really?'

'Yes. We used to go across from Liverpool to Dublin. From there we made a tour round Northern Ireland to Belfast, Coleraine, Londonderry, Donegal and down to Sligo, then across to Roscommon and Athlone and so to Galway. From there we did Ennis, Limerick and Waterford and came back to Dublin up the west coast.'

'What about Killarney?'

'That was a separate tour, but we still crossed from Liverpool to Dublin. We still do the Killarney tour, but not from Dublin. It's Swansea to Cork now, and then we go to Killarney by way of Macroom, tour the Ring of Kerry, go up as far as Tralee and then home again by way of Cork, Swansea, Llanelli (just to give the passengers a glimpse of South Wales) and that's their lot. On the outward journey we tip them off the coach at Swansea and in Eire the natives take over and an Irish courier takes the party round. We used to do the lot in the old Dublin days, but the Irish have taken over, so from our point of view the tour is not so profitable as it used to be.'

'What happens to the coach you take to Swansea?'

'Oh, the driver brings it straight back and we send it off on one of our shorter tours while the passengers are in Ireland, and pick them up again at Swansea on their return. Then they get their night at Llanelli and so home.'

'So the sight of one of your coaches down at the docks in Swansea would not occasion surprise to the port authorities or any other interested party?'

'Not on the first day it was there, and, of course, as for Daigh's coach, the Welsh police found it before anybody at the docks had even reported it was there.'

CHAPTER 4

Dantwylch, Below the Knoll

Dame Beatrice, having given her news and her views to Honfleur, prepared for her next inquisition. Having nothing to guide her except a list of names and addresses, she made what turned out to be an unhelpful choice of witnesses to the disappearance of Driver Daigh from the cathedral city of Dantwylch in West Wales, when, because one of them had a Welsh surname, she selected Miss Harvey and Mrs Williams, who had shared a seat and a twin-bedded room on the tour of the Pembrokeshire coast.

The two women were sisters and Londoners. There was a gap of ten years between their ages, Mrs Williams being the younger. She was a widow and, since the death of her husband five years previously, she and Miss Harvey had put their savings into the purchase and stock of a small general shop on the south coast where they did well enough to be able to take an annual holiday and pay a caretaker to manage the shop during the week that they were absent.

This caretaker was their brother's son, who was willing to give up a week of his own holiday to oblige his aunts and to make a little extra money on the side for himself. The shop was in Moordown, a suburb of Bournemouth, so he and his wife were able to spend Sunday at the seaside after he had taken the travellers on the Saturday morning to pick up their coach.

47

After much discussion, deliberation and consultation of various brochures, the sisters had decided to visit the land of Mrs Williams' deceased husband and, as had been the case on their previous coach tour, they intended to enjoy themselves.

'For everything's good for a laugh if you look at it the right way,' said Mrs Williams, upon whom her widowhood sat lightly. Her sister agreed and it was with blithe anticipation that they gave their modest suitcases into the care of the driver and settled into their seats.

The overnight stop was at Monmouth, where there was little time for the sisters to see anything much except the Monnow Bridge with its fortified gateway supporting a watchman's lodging, the statue of Henry V who was born in Monmouth Castle, and Goscombe John's bronze figure of C. S. Rolls, the motorist and aviator. These last two they ignored, knowing little of either.

So Miss Harvey and Mrs Williams went for a short stroll as far as the bridge when dinner was over and then they retired to their twin beds after what, for them, had been an exciting and somewhat tiring day. On the following morning the coach went by way of Abergavenny and Swansea, Llanelli and Carmarthen, to Tenby, where the party was to stay for three nights at a hotel on the cliff-top. Here Miss Harvey and Mrs Williams again were delighted with everything until later, when, with the rest of the passengers, they found themselves marooned in Dantwylch with neither coach nor driver.

The first full day in Tenby was given over to the coach-party to employ in any way it pleased. Lunch was provided at the hotel, from whose good position on the cliff-top there were views of the bay, the islands, the little harbour, the sea-girt rocks and a wide expanse of the sea itself.

Some of the passengers spent their time on the beach, although this involved a long trek down and a pretty steep climb up again. Others explored the town and admired the old walls. They visited the shops, the remains of the castle and even ventured into the small museum. The rest of the party went across to Caldy Island by motor-boat to view the Cistercian monastery and the remains of a Benedictine priory.

The second full day was to include a drive to Dantwylch to visit the Cathedral and the ruins of the bishop's palace.

'We haven't got much farther to go for our lunch,' said John Daigh, the coach-driver, when he had pulled up in the main street of Dantwylch near the traffic-free by-road which led down to the Cathedral and the ruins. 'There are two or three places nearby where you can get a cup of coffee and you'll have time for a bit of sightseeing, too. We leave here at exactly twelve noon, please. I'd like you all to be very punctual because I'm not allowed to hang about here. I can only set down and pick up. As soon as you are all off the coach I have to take it to the car park. If anybody doesn't get back to time, that's where we'll all have to go back and wait for stragglers, but it's a good walk away and it's uphill.' He laughed jovially and the passengers joined in. 'You won't want to miss me!' he assured them.

Most of them opted for coffee first and exploring afterwards, and Miss Harvey and Mrs Williams joined the majority in a small restaurant close at hand, having watched the coach drive away.

The sisters enjoyed their coffee, wended their way downhill, inspected the Cathedral with its shrine of the patron saint and walked as far as the entrance to the bishop's palace, but decided that they would not be able to spend enough time among the very extensive ruins to justify the charge for admission. They bought a leaflet 'just to show we've been,' and took the long, up-hill trek back to the bus-stop.

They were back far too soon, so they spent the time – killing it, to be more exact – in gazing in at nearby shop windows and in purchasing some sweets and a local newspaper. By dribs and drabs the rest of the coach-party joined them at the bus stop. The narrow pavement gradually became congested and a church clock struck twelve. Eyes were fixed expectantly on the road up which the coach had disappeared, but no coach came.

The church clock struck a disconsolate quarter; later, a warning half-hour. Still no coach appeared. The company became first restless, then agitated and at last angry. A policeman came up and one of the male passengers, abetted by others, told him of their dilemma. He suggested that one of them should go to the car-park and 'hurry the driver up a bit, because you are congesting the footway, look you.'

Two of the men took his advice, having received from the policeman explicit directions in order to reach the car-park by the shortest route. They returned at the end of twenty-five minutes with the stunning information that neither coach nor driver was to be found. The policeman then came to the rescue by alerting his inspector. That official, realising the importance of the tourist trade to his native town, made himself busy on the telephone and in an admirably short time a local coach pulled up, took the party on board and transported them to the hotel overlooking Fishguard harbour where they were booked in for lunch.

The hotel, which owed its very existence to the coach-parties who patronised it all through the summer months, coped efficiently and the local driver, having telephoned his employers and eaten the lunch intended for Driver Daigh, expressed his willingness to carry out the rest of the day's programme and to return the party to their hotel in Tenby in plenty of time for dinner.

At the dinner tables there was only one topic of conversation and only one viable solution of the mystery. The coach and its driver had been hijacked.

'Happens all the time,' ran the general consensus of opinion. 'Arabs or the Irish, most likely, or an escaped convict or someone.'

Miss Harvey and Mrs Williams were caught up in the general excitement, but, like most of the women, they felt a considerable amount of dismay.

'What's going to happen to the rest of the tour, and how are we going to get home?' they asked nervously.

'Oh, the company will send up another coach,' said an omniscient male. 'You don't want to worry. The receptionist here will have been on the telephone to them. We're supposed to have a trip to Aberystwyth and Devil's Bridge tomorrow, but, myself, I'd just as soon spend another day here in Tenby.'

The party did spend another day in Tenby. The hotel, it turned out, having received a telephone call from the Company's head office, arranged to give the passengers an unscheduled lunch, and before tea-time that afternoon a relief coach and its driver had turned up, and the party was conveyed to Towyn, where it was to spend the night. The rest of the tour, apart from continued speculation and surmise and an unprecedented sale of papers 'in case we should be in the news', continued as per programme.

'We don't let them down,' said Honfleur, somewhat smugly, later, to Dame Beatrice.

'We couldn't understand it at all,' said Mrs Williams, the more personable and therefore, perhaps, the more forthcoming of the two. 'It needs some looking into, that it does.'

'I am here to look into it,' said Dame Beatrice, already beginning to regret her choice of witnesses.

'We heard there was another coach, before ours, that had something happen to it,' said Mrs Williams.

'It lost its driver, yes. This was not your first coach tour, I am told.'

'Nor it was with most of the people on the tour. Most had been before.'

Dame Beatrice nodded.

'I wonder whether you had any premonitions, before you left the coach to go sight-seeing in Dantwylch, that something untoward was going to happen?' she enquired.

This inviting and leading question was to test the suggestibility and therefore, to some extent, the reliability of the witnesses. The sisters, true to their Cockney origin, stood firm.

'Of course not,' said Miss Harvey, 'else we should have stayed behind in Tenby.'

'Could you give me a short account of exactly what happened that day at Dantwylch?'

Like schoolchildren asked to describe a day in their summer holidays, the sisters, sometimes interrupting and very occasionally contradicting one another, began their account.

'We got up after we'd made a cup of tea with the electric machine which another lady had shown us how to manage the night before, had a nice wash and then we went downstairs. I had grapefruit juice and bacon and egg and Maud had orange juice and a plate of cornflakes . . .'

'Porridge, that day, Carrie.'

'Oh, yes, that's right, porridge. After that she had bacon and sausage and a fried tomato, and we finished up with toast and marmalade, because I said as the bread rolls would be too filling if we had cakes at the coffee shop and our lunch to come. Besides, rolls is more fattening nor toast, though I will say as they put plenty of butter on the table . . .'

'And there was two kinds of marmalade, the chunky and the shred . . .'

'And honey. Don't forget the honey. All in them individual little pots, so convenient and giving fair shares for everybody.'

'Better than that, because there was six pots between four of us, but, of course, we only took one pot each . . .'

'And I finished yours up, you not liking too much marmalade on top of your butter and me not liking to waste good food.'

At last Dame Beatrice got them to describe the journey itself and their experiences in Dantwylch.

'Can you remember the last words you heard the driver say?' she asked, at the end of another pointless recital.

'Not word for word, but it was clear enough,' said Mrs Williams. 'He was putting us down so we could have a coffee and a walk round, and we was to be back in the same place at twelve sharp 'cos he wasn't allowed to hang about for us. If anybody was late back, he'd wait for them in the car-park further up the hill. But nobody *was* late back and we all hung about there for more than half the day, all told. We was just mooching around and looking at the shops, but not liking to go far away in case the coach turned up while we was gone. My feet ached, because it was a fair old climb up from the Cathedral, and not all that much to see when you got inside. Dark, I mean, and, to my mind, not so good as Christchurch Priory.' Mrs Williams seemed prepared to go on, but Dame Beatrice prevented this.

"You had stopped for lunch in Swansea on your second day out. Did the driver give any indication that he knew anybody or had any friends there?'

'Swansea? What about it? Oh – *Swansea*. You mean because that's where they found our coach?'

'Yes. Did the driver appear to make any contacts there?'

The sisters shook their heads.

'He never said nothing about knowing nobody there, not in particular,' said Mrs Williams. 'He knew the hotel, of course. Good food, but very crowded it was. He knew the hotel because he'd taken coach parties there before. It was the coaches' usual lunch stop and right in the middle of the town. The dining room was so full that some of our gentlemen had a job to get hold of anybody to bring a glass of beer to the table and there hadn't been no time to go into the bar. At table there wasn't hardly elbow-room to use your knife and fork. I had a steak. Maud, you had the plaice, didn't you?'

'So the driver knew the hotel, but you do not think he had friends in the town,' said Dame Beatrice. 'Let us return to Dantwylch. What happened at the end of your long wait for the coach which did not return to pick you up?'

'A policeman come up and one or two of the gentlemen explained what had happened.'

'And then?'

'He sent two of them up to the car-park, but, of course, Mr Daigh and the coach wasn't there. Funny you should ask about friends in the town, though, now I come to think of it. Mind you, we thought he was only joking, but he did say, pulling our legs, like, mine and my sister's (very pleasant he always made himself to everybody), he *did* say as he might be picking up his girl-friend in Dantwylch. "And her trousseau," he said. "Funny, some of the things these women like," he said. Then he laughed, very pleasant he was, and off we went to Dantwylch and, of course, we never see him again once he'd drove off to the car park. I was real sorry, I can tell you.'

'Did the two gentlemen find out whether the coach had ever reached the car park?'

'Oh, yes. It had got there all right, but it wasn't there when they arrived. There was two other coaches, they said, but not ours. They spoke to the drivers, but they couldn't tell them nothing.'

'Can you remember their names?'

'Our two gentlemen, do you mean? One was Mr Ames. I don't know the other one's name. He was travelling on his own, I think, wasn't he, Maud? Mr Ames was married, but the other gentleman . . .'

'Nice and polite, but kept to himself except at the table,' said Miss Harvey. 'Nobody couldn't keep to theirselves there, because of the numbers, you see.'

'But the other coach drivers had seen your coach come in, had they?'

'No, but they'd seen it drive out. They didn't think nothing of it, because they thought our driver was going off to pick us up, but, of course, it was much too early for that. It wouldn't have been no more than about eleven o'clock, they said.'

Slightly wearied by the witnesses, Dame Beatrice went to Mr Ames' address. He was at work, but his wife was at home.

'He can't tell you anything more than I can,' she said. 'We've discussed it over and over. I'm glad the Company's doing something about it as well as the police. The last we heard of Mr Daigh, he was going to pick us up again at twelve. I wanted coffee and the Cathedral, but Tom thought better of a pub, so I went with him, of course, and never saw the Cathedral at all, but when some of them told me what a long climb up it had been I was glad I hadn't gone.'

'So at what time did you and your husband return to the picking-up place?'

'Oh, not until just on twelve. Tom said there wasn't any point and it was a very nice pub, so we got into conversation and stopped on.'

'And then you waited for your coach, but it did not materialise.'

'That's right. Very put out we all were. Well, I mean, you don't pay that sort of money to waste time hanging about on your holiday and being jostled on the pavement, do you?'

'What had your husband to say about his visit to the coach station?'

'The policeman suggested it, so he and Mr Mellick went, but it wasn' any good. They asked around and there was no doubt our coach had been there, because another coach driver had seen it drive off.'

'With nobody in it except for Mr Daigh, I suppose?'

'He was sure there was nobody but the driver, and who else *could* have been in it? We were all turned out of it down in the town. Nobody stayed on it. Sometimes they do, at the coffee stops, but not this time.'

'Did your husband speak to anybody else who had actually seen Mr Daigh?'

'Oh, yes. He and Mr Mellick spoke to the man on the exit barrier. The car-park is sort of automatic, you see. You drive up and snatch a parking card from an automatic machine and the barrier lifts and lets you through. Then when you leave there's a little sort of office and you hand in your card and the parking fee to the man and he pulls a lever that raises the barrier to let you out. It's to prevent cars being stolen from the car-park, you see. You can't take your car out without you can produce your card.'

'It sounds an excellent system.'

'Oh, we've had it for years in Poole, where I come from, only *our* car-park is multi-storey,' said the witness complacently.

'So, at Dantwylch, nobody in authority need be aware that a car or a coach has come in, but there is always a check on a vehicle going out?'

'That's right. The man on the barrier remembered our coach perfectly, and, near enough, the time.'

'Oh, he noticed the time, did he?'

'Eleven o'clock, give or take five minutes, he told my husband.'

'Did he mention whether he recognised the driver?'

'He didn't say. Not that it would have done much good to ask, I don't suppose. There's a lot of shift-work, I dare say, in these car-parks, especially in holiday places. Long hours, you see. You couldn't have one man on duty all the time. Like enough he wouldn't have recognised Mr Daigh unless he'd just happened to be on duty the other times the coach parked there on the Pembroke tour.'

'And there was no suggestion that more than one man was in the coach, I suppose?'

'Nobody asked. Well, as I said, there couldn't have been, could there? We all got off the coach at the bus stop where Mr Daigh set us down.'

'He might have picked up somebody in the car-park, I suppose – somebody he knew and who had asked him for a lift.'

'What! A lift into Swansea when we were due to be picked up in an hour's time to go to lunch in Fishguard? Surely he wouldn't have been so silly! Even if he was, well, I mean, why wasn't he with the coach when the police found it? He was hi-jacked, that's what my husband says.'

CHAPTER 5

The Bishop's Palace

Following almost but not quite the same procedure as in Derbyshire, this time Dame Beatrice took her secretary with her and left her chauffeur at home. Laura was a first-class driver and, in any case, was what she herself described as 'mad to get in on the man-hunt' which she regarded as more of a holiday spree than a serious quest.

They followed the route taken by Driver Daigh's coach-party, but stayed only one night at Tenby following the night at Monmouth. Laura commented upon the Monnow bridge.

'Pity there's no access to the public,' she said, eyeing the structure with its fort-like aspect. 'If people are allowed up into the porter's lodging over the Westgate at Winchester, I don't see why we can't be allowed the same sort of access to the lodging over the Monnow bridge.'

'The pavement is narrow. There might be congestion and foot-passengers not wishing to visit the lodging might be forced into the road, don't you think?'

'Well, I find this a tantalising town,' said Laura. 'I got up early this morning and went to look at the castle where H. Five was born. There's very little of it left, and what there is appears to be on land which belongs to the military.'

They lunched at the hotel and then, without stopping at Swansea, made for the hotel at Tenby where the coach-party had stayed for three nights. Enquiries there led to nothing and both the receptionist and the manager proved a trifle restive, already, they stated, having been questioned exhaustively by the police.

Dame Beatrice and Laura remained there for the night and early on the following morning they set out for Dantwylch and drove straight to the car-park. Here they met with the same kind of reception as they had experienced in Tenby. However, Dame Beatrice's questions were answered civilly enough, although no fresh information was forthcoming and the man on duty at the exit could give no description of the County Motors driver.

'So now back to Swansea, I suppose,' said Laura, 'although it seems a pity not to take a look at the Cathedral while we're here.'

'And the ruins of the bishop's palace,' agreed Dame Beatrice. 'We have plenty of time before we go off for lunch.'

The Cathedral detained them for half an hour. Dame Beatrice purchased a handbook and studied it while she sat in a pew. Laura poked around and identified the various architectural periods beginning with the Norman mouldings of the nave arcade and ending with the modern statue of the patron saint with the Celtic dove of eloquence perched upon his shoulder.

When Laura had looked also at the fifteenth century misericords on the choir stalls, studied the shrine of the saint with its rearward holes for pilgrims' offerings, seen the early fifteenth-century carvings which formed part of the canopy of the bishop's stall, she and Dame Beatrice left the Cathedral, crossed the water, came to the gatehouse of the bishop's palace, paid the entrance fee and passed into the courtyard.

The ruins were vast and imposing. From the hut just inside the outer courtyard where they had taken tickets and bought a descriptive, illustrated brochure, Laura, delighted with the size and complexity of the place, began her exploration.

Dame Beatrice stayed and chatted with the man on duty at the hut, for there were few visitors that morning, as no coach-parties had yet arrived. People came from all over the country, he averred. The ruins were the finest in Britain, although he confessed that he had seen no others. Yes, there were two halls, as was stated in the brochure. One had been for the bishop's own use, look you, and the other was for important persons, some of them not too nice, no, indeed, not from all he had read of them, but important, oh, yes, very important, no doubt.

No, the gatehouse was never closed. Who would want to visit the ruins after dark? Even if they did, there was little damage they could do and a good chance of breaking their necks on the outside steps or on the newel staircases.

Yes, it was all open to the public during the daytime except the porter's room over the gate. That had been bricked up in — when was it now? — oh, yes, in the wartime, because, although the roof had gone, the upper floor remained. If there were traitors about, or enemy agents, it could have been used as a signalling base to enemy aircraft.

'Right over on this west side of the country?' Dame Beatrice sceptically enquired. She was asked what a hundred or so miles meant to an aeroplane and was told that in time of war no safety measure was out of place.

'Then is the fabric never inspected?' she asked. 'What if the gatehouse itself were unsafe?'

Oh, the Department of the Environment would see to that. A regular check was kept on all the historic buildings, yes, indeed. It would not be fair to the public, who paid to visit the ruins, if their safety was not looked to. Very bad that would be, and bad, too, for the tourist trade. Dame Beatrice nodded sympathetically in agreement with all this.

A couple more visitors turned up at this point, so Dame Beatrice walked across the courtyard and inspected the long, vaulted undercroft whose top storey had disappeared. Then, faced by a steep stone stair which led up to the great hall, she gazed at it, but did not mount. She walked along the front of the buildings, and from the plan and photographs in the brochure

she identified the rest of the ruins and then seated herself on one
of the steps which led up to the bishop's hall, his kitchen at one
end and his solar and chapel at the other, and prepared to wait
for Laura.

The plan, which she continued to study, suggested that, at one
time, there had been access to the porter's room from the chapel,
but, according to the brochure, that was indeed now blocked.
She read on until Laura came back, delighted with everything.

'Four newel staircases im the thickness of the walls, two outside stairs, three wall-fireplaces – the great hall must have had a
central hearth, I should think – barrel vaulting, some decorated
tracery in two of the windows and there's a kitchen hatch opening on to a long corridor so that food could be taken to both of
the halls.

'There are some gorgeous carvings of grotesque stone heads,
used, I suppose, as corbels to support a floor which has gone,
and I spotted two garderobes, although there must have been
more. You don't seem to have poked about much. Weren't you
interested?'

'Immensely so, but climbing down newel staircases, and
mounting outer ones which have no handrail, does not appeal to
me. I have talked to the man who issues tickets of admission and
have made a close study of the plan which is in the handbook. I
have also looked at the gatehouse.'

'Yes, but, same as at Monmouth, there's no admission to the
porter's room. You can see where the opening from the chapel
has been closed up, though, and I noticed that what must have
been the entrance to a staircase on the inside wall of the
gatehouse has also been blocked off. What interested you
specially?'

'Merely random thoughts.'

Laura looked at her suspiciously.

'Oh, yes?' she said. 'Too random to be recollected in tran-
quillity?'

'Perhaps I should have called them *idle* thoughts. Moreover, they were primarily your responsibility. Twice, on this pilgrimage of ours, we have passed under gatehouse archways. Each supports a room which is closed to the public. But for you, I should not have thought twice about these facts, but, now that my attention has been drawn to them, I find them interesting.'

'Why?'

'I was wondering what has become of Driver Daigh.'

'The man we're chasing? Well, we both wonder about him, I suppose.'

'Yes. I see that the custodian is at liberty again, so I will venture to accost him once more.' She walked across the courtyard to the little kiosk. 'I suppose you get coach-parties every day in summer,' she said, when she had purchased half-a-dozen picture postcards of the ruins.

'Not every day, perhaps, but most days.'

'I suppose their drivers come with them and show them round?'

'Oh, no, indeed. A driver would be taking the coach to the car park and having a good talk with other drivers and getting himself a cup of coffee, maybe. No, I never knew a driver to come down here. Drivers don't care about walking, look you, and having a stiff climb up a lot of steps to the top. Oh, the drivers wouldn't trouble themselves, not they. And the people off the coaches, go into the Cathedral they do — no charge for that, see? — but not so many come on here, not nearly so many as you would suppose. Admission charge, you see, and not much time to have a good look round, anyway, by the time they've had their coffee and seen the Cathedral.'

'So now for Swansea, I suppose,' said Laura, when they left the ruins.

'No, I think not. The police will have made exhaustive enquires there and, in any case, I believe that the appearance of Daigh's coach in Swansea was intended to deceive.'

'What makes you think so?'

'It was all too obvious that the police were intended to think that something or someone was shipped over from Swansea to Cork. It is the route by which this particular company conveys its passengers when they take their tour of Southern Ireland.'

'Well, why shouldn't the police think so? They might be right.'

'The effort to deceive often defeats its own purpose. Let us lunch, as the coach party did, at the hotel overlooking Fishguard Bay. It is very well situated, I am told, and I have the name of it from Mr Honfleur.'

The view from the terrace of the hotel was spacious and beautiful. Below it was the bay. The sea, calm in its sheltered inlet, reflected the blue sky. A rocky promontory at the entrance to the harbour stood out black against the afternoon brightness. Immediately below the terrace the steep slope of the hill was green and gold and there were wild flowers among the grasses. A lane wound away past the hotel seawards down a slope which began a gradual descent and then steepened. Laura, after lunch, walked a little way down it, but soon trees and tall bushes hid the harbour and she returned to the front of the hotel where she had left Dame Beatrice in contemplation of the view.

'What now?' she asked. Dame Beatrice waved a yellow claw.

'The boat from Rosslare is just coming in,' she said. 'A good lunch, did you not think? Also, if I mistake not, here comes a motor-coach party. I would prefer to retain our privacy and peace. Shall we return by way of Hereford? I booked rooms there for tonight.'

'And we're really not going to Swansea?'

'And we really are not going to Swansea. I must speak to Mr Honfleur again, and as soon as I can.'

'But you've nothing to report, have you?'

'I shall say that we made no enquiries in Swansea.'

Laura gave it up. They got into the car and headed for Carmarthen and Brecon.

It was impossible to leave Hereford next morning without visiting the Cathedral, so it was not until half-past ten that Dame

Beatrice and Laura left the hotel. When they were headed for Winchester Dame Beatrice said,

'I have a strange yearning to inspect the Westgate ahead of us.'

'Haven't you seen it before?'

'Only the exterior.'

'May I ask why this sudden enthusiasm?'

'Because I have often suspected you of possessing second sight, and, as I told you, it is you who have directed my attention to gatehouses.'

Laura, who often suspected her employer of laughing at her, disdained to continue the conversation. She parked the car as near the Westgate as the regulations allowed and together they ascended the flight of stone steps which led up to a vast door. The room they entered was furnished as a tiny museum and behind a table sat the curator.

'There is a way up to the roof, if you wish,' he said. Laura guessed that this roof was their objective, but they looked at the exhibits in what had been the thirteenth-century gatekeeper's lodging and then they climbed a second staircase, a shorter one this time, and stepped out into the open air.

The parapet was crenellated with alternate embrasures and merlons. Dame Beatrice regarded it with approval, while Laura went from side to side of the flat roof to obtain the views.

'What next, then?' she asked, when she had done this.

'Home, when I have telephoned Henri that we shall arrive in time for dinner. The afternoon is yet young. Let us walk alongside the delightful River Itchen wherein an acquaintance of mine once assured me that he had seen a naiad. We will go as far as St Cross, a modest mile or so away, and hope to see a kingfisher or maybe a wily trout as we wander across the water-meadows.'

On the following morning, chauffeur-driven, this time, by her man-servant George, Dame Beatrice went to report to Basil Honfleur.

'So you did not go to Swansea,' said Honfleur, when they met.

'I thought it unnecessary. All the possible enquiries there have been made by the police.'

'Yes, well, naturally I've had to answer their questions. It seems that the port authorities are accustomed to seeing our coaches in the parking lot, and thought nothing of it when Daigh's coach arrived.'

'But did they expect it to stay so long?'

'The police asked them that and they said it was unusual, but they weren't worried. The point is, as I told you, that an Irish coach takes over when our passengers reach Cork. The tour really starts from there.'

'With an Irish driver, I think you said.'

'Oh, yes. You'll remember that our man brings our coach back here so that it can be used for one of our shorter tours while the passengers are over in Ireland. Then it returns to Swansea in time to pick them up again. It takes them to Llanelli for the night, because the boat does not get in very early. They're due for an extra dinner, bed and breakfast, anyway, before we bring them back here. Besides, it's a lovely drive on the last day. They come by way of the Severn Bridge, and feel they're getting a bonus.'

'Tell me, where would you hide a murdered body, should you chance to have such an incubus about you?'

'Murdered? You don't think these poor chaps of mine have been *murdered*?'

'Your affectation of astonishment does not deceive me. Our first conversation convinced me that you yourself already feared as much.'

"Only because I couldn't think of any other reason for their disappearance. I never mentioned murder, did I?'

'I do not remember, but it was clear to me that you had murder in mind.'

'Well, they were such good chaps, you see. I couldn't imagine them just walking out on their jobs, let alone on their wives and children.'

'Have they wives and children?'

'Now that you ask me, I must confess that I've no idea.'

'You suggested, I remember – or somebody did – that they might have domestic troubles.'

'Oh, well, now! After all, their domestic complications are no business of mine.'

'Oh, quite. No doubt the police have made that sort of enquiry their affair, if only to be sure of getting the bodies identified if my fears prove to be justified.'

'Look here, you're hinting at all sorts of horrible things. What *do* you think has happened? You're holding out on me, aren't you? You know something you haven't told me.'

'It is not knowledge. It is merely surmise. Moreover, it takes me back to a question which, so far, you have not answered.'

'Where would I hide a murdered body? That is if I had been the murderer, I assume.'

'The murderer or his accomplice.'

'Are you serious?'

'On this occasion, yes.'

'You're thinking of Derbyshire, I suppose. Well, there's plenty of space on the moors.'

'And in West Wales?'

'Oh, I don't know, but there must be plenty of places. I suppose it would depend upon how quickly one wanted to get rid of the body.'

'Yes, no doubt a great deal would depend upon that.'

'Look, what are you getting at?'

'I hardly know.'

'Well, I know this much: you wouldn't be talking like this unless you had something to go on. Why don't you tell me what it is?'

'Because I do not trust your walls.'

'Good God, they're not bugged!'

'No, but they are said to have ears.'

'You don't trust my drivers?'

'I am not sure that I have ever fully trusted anybody except Laura and my servants.'

'But that's a terrible philosophy!'

'Not at all. Remember what Gilbert Keith Chesterton said.'

'About what?'

' "Blessed is he that expecteth nothing, for he shall be gloriously surprised." '

'Well, suppose *you* surprise *me,* and not necessarily gloriously. What *are* you getting at? Let's go outside if you don't want to talk here.'

'We could talk in my car.' They went out to it and took the back seat. 'Drive us around a little, George,' said Dame Beatrice to her chauffeur. Then, as they moved into a stream of traffic, she settled herself as though she had no more to say.

'Well?' said Honfleur at last. His query was answered by another.

'I have it from you that Noone and Daigh were efficient drivers, but what kind of men were they?'

'I've already told you that I know nothing of their private lives.'

'I am not thinking of them as husbands and fathers, but as comrades and fellow-workers. You have indicated that your driver-couriers are closely knit. Were Noone and Daigh any different from the rest?'

'No, not in that way. They got on well with everybody, so far as I know.'

'Apart from the other drivers, who must be weary of police interrogations, have you any other employees who would know something about these two men?'

'Oh, I expect a certain amount of chatting-up and chaff goes on between our drivers and the two women behind the counter in our main booking hall. Any cancellations, you see, come in by telephone (often at the last minute, unfortunately for us), and are taken by the counter clerks. It's then their business to contact me or my secretary and then to inform the drivers.'

'I should like to talk with one of these young ladies.'

'Not so awfully young, actually. Mrs Wade has been with us ten years and Miss Morley for seven.'

'That is splendid. If they have been subjected to chat and chaff for those lengths of time, they must have formed some definite opinions about your various men.'

'Oh, I expect so. Anyway, talk to them by all means. At this time in the season they were unlikely to be very busy, as practically all the bookings will have been made, so there will be little except cancellations to be dealt with.'

Dame Beatrice interviewed Mrs Wade first, and across her counter, as though it was an enquiry about travel. Mrs Wade was a cheerful, plump, pretty woman in her mid-thirties, accustomed, because of her job, to answering questions and retaining a helpful demeanour. Such evidence as she could offer was independently reinforced by Miss Morley at a separate interview which took place just outside the booking hall.

'Cyril Noone was a quiet fellow. Not much to say for himself, but would do anything for anybody.'

'Including, perhaps, giving a stranger a lift in his coach when his passengers were out of it?' Dame Beatrice enquired.

'Oh, not casual strangers, of course. But if there was another coach-driver in trouble, especially one of our lot or even a man working for another tour company, Cyril would do his best to help him out, I'm sure, provided it didn't hold up the tour at all.'

'What about Mr. Daigh?'

'Well, he was a different sort. Fond of his joke, but never nasty or embarrassing with it. Quite the gentleman in that sort of way, but – well, you know – liked his bit of fun.'

'Gentlemanly enough to take a sick person to hospital, for example? Someone who was not on the tour, I mean.'

'Oh, I couldn't quite say that. The coaches are on a very tight schedule, you see. There wouldn't be time for a driver to go off like that, although I'd say that, in the ordinary way, I'm sure Jack Daigh would do a good turn if he died for it.'

'Which he may well have done,' said Dame Beatrice, when she recounted to Laura the information she had received from the desk-clerks.

'So what will you do now?' asked Laura.

'I shall return to Derbyshire and talk to the County police. I have no doubt that they will have searched the moors. The search must be unsuccessful, or we should have heard. I shall suggest a different hiding-place for poor Noone's body. If my suggestion is well received and their search of my rather unlikely hiding-place is successful, then I shall convey the same suggestion to the police who are conducting the search for Daigh in Wales.'

'But what is this long shot of yours?'

'I prefer not to say until I know whether or not it has reached its target.'

'And you do really think that these missing drivers have been murdered? But why?'

'Why do I think so? – or why have they been murdered?'

'Both, I suppose.'

'I think so because *you* think so. Isn't that right?'

'Perhaps it is. It's the fact that *two* are missing which bothers me.'

'As for why they have been murdered, well, the temporary theft of the Welsh coach – if a theft can be held to be temporary – indicates a robbery of a more serious kind, I think.'

'You mean our coach was commandeered to convey stolen goods?' asked Honfleur incredulously when she made the suggestion to him.

'It is a reasonable supposition, I think. I wonder why *you* think so?'

'Oh, I don't! I think you're jumping to conclusions far too readily. What kind of stolen goods would need a coach to transport them?'

'Thousands of cigarettes, cases of contraband liquor, a fortune in narcotics wrapped up in bales of textiles ... or even an innocent-seeming suitcase.'

'Oh, all right! But we've no details of such stolen cargoes, have we?'

'*We* have not, but what about the police?'

'The police? Well, so far as we are concerned, all they know at present is that two of our drivers are missing. That's all I care about. In any case, your theories of theft and murder still have to be proved. How do you propose to set about it? Have you really any ideas?'

'I shall go back to Derbyshire and talk with the Chief Constable of the district in which Driver Noone disappeared. If he will agree to do as I ask, one of my theories — well, not theories so much as wild guesses, I fear — will either be proved or disproved. If I am right, and we find Noone, then I know where to find Daigh.'

'And it's of no use to ask you any more questions?'

'At present, no. I am probably going on a wild-goose chase and a ridiculous one at that, and if it weren't for Laura I should not be undertaking it at all.'

'*I* suggested it?' exclaimed Laura.

'No. You simply and quite unintentionally put a grotesque thought into my head.'

CHAPTER 6

Devil-Porter It No Further

The Chief Constable of the district in which Hulliwell Hall was situated looked dubious.

'But what makes you think so?' he asked. 'A body on a gatehouse roof? It seems such a fantastic idea.'

'In Monmouth my secretary remarked on the fact that there appears to be no admission to the watchman's lodging which forms part of the fourteenth century Monnow bridge.'

'But Monmouth doesn't come into the matter, except that County Coaches stay there one night on their Welsh tours, but their Welsh tours are nothing to do with us.'

'After that, I discovered that, although there used to be a way in and out of the room at the top of the gatehouse to the bishop's palace at Dantwylch, the passage between that and the ruins of the chapel has been bricked up for years.'

'I still don't follow. In any case, what have I to do with all that?'

'Then I inspected the roof over the watchman's dwelling on the Westgate at Winchester. The parapet there would conceal anybody who crouched or was lying down on the roof. This, all of it, made me think of the gatehouse which forms the entrance to your Hulliwell Hall.'

'I think this is all rather far-fetched, you know, Dame Beatrice.'

'You have searched the moors, you say.'

'Exhaustively, but it doesn't mean that there aren't dozens of hiding places we could have missed. We've even had a helicopter out, but you can't see into all the holes and crevices. There are stone-quarries, tumble-down drystone walls, disused sheep-pens, limestone caverns – any number of hiding-places and hazards. Besides, you're going on the assumption that these men are dead. We don't admit that. We shall continue to do our best to find them, of course, but, as we pointed out to the coach people when they made their first report, men do walk out of their own accord and are quite skilful at covering their tracks. Honestly, Dame Beatrice, don't you think that is the case here?'

'I might very well think so if only one coach-driver had been missing, but the disappearance of two of them within such a short space of time gives one food for thought.'

'Well, yes, I suppose it does, but coincidences are not so very unusual and both men may have become tired of their jobs with the tour company, talked it over with one another and decided to quit.'

'One in Derbyshire and one in West Wales?'

'Well, two men roaming together would be more conspicuous than if each man went off on his own. We've circulated a description of Noone and the Welsh police, with whom we're in contact, have done the same for Daigh. Now we and they have combined and issued both descriptions in case the men *have* teamed up somewhere or other. I don't see what more we can do, except continue with routine enquiries.'

'Did your helicopter fly over Hulliwell Hall?'

'Over the surrounding countryside it did, but there isn't much cover there. It was the moorland terrain which we searched most thoroughly for hiding-places, but we've made lots of house to house enquiries as well, you know. We particularly asked whether anybody in the village saw anything suspicious or had taken in a lodger, for example, at about the time in question.'

'I wish you would get your men to inspect the gatehouse at

the Hall. Would that be too difficult to arrange?'

'Well, no, I suppose not. The owners are away and I know the fellow who is agent for the estate. It can be managed if you're especially keen on it. Nothing will come of it, you know.'

'I do not expect anything to come of it, but it would oblige me very much if the roof of that gatehouse could be eliminated, as it were, from my list of suspected hiding-places for a body.'

'Very well, but I think you're looking for a mare's nest.'

'That may be so, but I always pay attention to my secretary's observations. She has Highland blood and sometimes that brings with it the unenviable gift of second sight.'

'Oh, come, now, Dame Beatrice! You will not persuade me that you indulge in superstitions of that sort!'

'To give some credence to the theory that extra-sensory perceptions do exist is not superstition. Besides, Laura has not claimed that Noone's body is on the top of the gatehouse at Hulliwell Hall. She merely drew my attention to the fact that some of these defensive structures which were erected by our ancestors to keep out unwelcome visitors no longer offer admittance to the porter's lodging and watch-tower.'

'There must be arrangements to have the fabric inspected from time to time. The body, if one was there —'

'When was the gatehouse at Hulliwell Hall last inspected, I wonder?' said Dame Beatrice.

'Oh, well,' said the Chief Constable, good-humouredly, 'that will certainly give me a talking-point with Hutchings. He lives on the estate in what used to be the dower house. I'll ring him up. If nothing else, he will be charmed to meet you. He loves celebrities.'

It was Mrs Hutchings who answered the telephone. Her husband, she explained, was up at the Hall, where some workmen were repairing part of the stonework balustrade of the terrace. He would be back at tea-time. Would the Chief Constable (she called him Tom) bring Dame Beatrice along for a cup of tea and a chat? She and Hugh would be delighted to meet her.

The gatehouse? Oh, of course it was safe! If Dame Beatrice would like to see the view from the top, that could easily be arranged. The Hall was closed to tourists at six, so perhaps, when she had been shown over the gatehouse, Dame Beatrice might like to see some of those parts of the Hall which were not open to the public. Yes, if they would care to come along at about half-past four, Hugh should be in by then.

Hutchings turned out to be more than willing to show Dame Beatrice any part of the mansion she would like to see. The gatehouse? Oh, was she particularly interested in gatehouses? Had she seen the whacking great structure at Thornton Abbey and the charming little entrance to South Wraxall Manor? Then there was the mighty fortification on the house side of the moat at Kirkby Muxloe, and one of his own favourites was the half-timbered, cottage-style gatehouse at Lower Brockhampton Hall.

'But, then, I'm a Chester man,' he said. The conversation turned on to a comparison of Chester and York and might have continued indefinitely but for Mrs Hutchings' reminder to her husband of his promise to show Dame Beatrice the view from the gatehouse roof.

The dower house was separated from the Hall by about half a mile of park-land, the evening was mellow and it still wanted a couple of hours to sunset, so the three set off on foot and approached the gatehouse from the inside. The cash customers who had come as sightseers had all been shepherded away, but the man on duty was still in his little kiosk checking the takings against the number of tickets sold that day. Hutchings greeted him and told him that he was taking the two visitors up to the roof to look at the view.

On the outer side of the archway a stout door had to be unlocked. Hutchings was carrying an electric torch, for the newel stair which they mounted was lighted only by one slit of a window and there was no handrail.

The porter's room was tiny compared with that above the

Westgate at Winchester, but here, again, there was access to the roof and the soft, clear evening light. Hutchings had led the way up the winding stair, but when Dame Beatrice had made a brief survey, by the light of an electric torch, of the tiny, stone-walled room, she was the first to mount to the leads.

She stood aside at the top of the short, steep, straight flight of steps so that the way was not blocked for her companions, and as they joined her on the small, flat roof she said,

'Just as well that we are in the open air.'

'You *must* have known,' said the Chief Constable, visiting Dame Beatrice at the Dovedale hotel on the following morning.

'No,' Dame Beatrice responded. 'It fell out just as I told you. Laura had this obsession about gatehouses and they did seem to offer possibilities as hiding-places. It has been pointed out, more than once, that to commit a murder is easy enough. It is the disposal of the body which presents the problem. Some bury the victim's corpse in somebody else's grave; others burn it; some dismember it and strew the remains over as wide an area as possible; others are content to dispose only of the head in the hope that the rest of the cadaver will defy recognition and identification; and there is also a school of thought which favours placing the remains in the left-luggage offices at railway stations and destroying the incriminating reclamation ticket. It was left to the fertile imagination of my secretary to envisage the possibilities of mediaeval gatehouses.'

'Your secretary may have been obsessed by gatehouses, but I don't believe she thought of them as repositories for murdered bodies. That was *your* idea, Dame Beatrice. Well, you may as well make up your mind to stay on here for a day or two. You will be needed at the inquest. Mind you, we shall soon get the fellow who did this,' said the Chief Constable.

'You think so?'

'Bound to. Nobody could have got a dead body up that newel

stair. It's so narrow that I had quite a job to squeeze myself up, and I was carrying nothing but an electric torch. The chap or chaps must have had a ladder and reared it up to the gatehouse roof from outside. What's more, they must have killed poor Noone – we must get the body formally identified, of course, but I have no doubt myself that it's Noone – they must have killed him somewhere else while the coach-party was inside Hulliwell Hall. Then they brought the body back to the gatehouse by night and in a car. It will be hard luck if we can't get a line on something there, because, as I say, they must also have brought a ladder. Well, you've certainly led us to discover the body. We should never have thought of that gatehouse for ourselves. Now the inquest —'

'Could I not be represented as a casual visitor taken up, as you told the gatekeeper, merely to admire the view from the gatehouse roof? It would accord better with my plans if the discovery of the body appeared to be fortuitous. I don't want gatehouses brought too obviously into the picture. I know I was the first person to set eyes on the body, but it was only a matter of seconds before you and Mr Hutchings saw it, too. You will remember that I stood aside immediately I had stepped out on to the roof so that you and he might join me.'

'I see what you mean. Anyway, we shall hold the inquest as soon as we can get the body identified. Not a very nice job for whoever it is. Let's hope the poor devil was a bachelor. I'd hate a woman to have to do it.'

'We both are going on the assumption that the body is that of Noone, and I think it a fair assumption, considering all that we know, but what if that particular identification fails?'

'That will make a nuisance for us, of course, but the body was completely clad and the poor fellow had a pretty full set of false teeth which should be identifiable if we chase around long enough to find the dentist who supplied them. One of the more tedious jobs for my chaps, but one which usually brings results. However, my bet is that we've found Noone all right. As you

say, given all the circumstances, I shouldn't think there's any
doubt about it.'

'No, I do not think there is any doubt at all.'

Papers found on the body identified it as that of Noone and the
inquest, which Dame Beatrice decided, after all, to attend, made
public the manner of the driver's death. He had been stabbed in
the back.

'One blow, but whoever did it either knew exactly where to
put the knife or else accidentally hit upon just the right spot,'
said the Chief Constable, discussing the inquest later. 'Could be
a Mafia job, but why pick on this particular chap? Wonder what
his political affiliations were? He wasn't an Irishman, was he? –
although they generally shoot their victims, not stab to kill. Was
he Jewish, I wonder, and some Arab terrorists got him? Was
any one of the coach-party involved? Oh, well, there are a
number of lines my chaps can follow up, and that's always
something. As the coach-party came from all over the place,
perhaps we ought to get Scotland Yard on to it. I'll see what my
Detective Chief Superintendent thinks. There's the Welsh job as
well, you see. There must be some connection. Do you expect to
find Daigh's body in the same kind of situation?'

'Well, there certainly is a gatehouse at the entrance to the
bishop's outer courtyard at Dantwylch,' said Dame Beatrice. 'I
noted that the medical evidence mentioned traces of soil in
Noone's hair,' she added, with apparent inconsequence. 'I think
the unfortunate man was persuaded to pick up his murderer outside Hulliwell Hall and take him some short distance, perhaps
towards a public house or a garage. On the way the murderer
stabbed the unsuspecting man in the back and ...'

'But the coach would have been filthy with blood. Nobody
has mentioned anything of that sort, have they?' asked the Chief
Constable.

'Presumably because there was *not* anything of that sort. You
would need to ask the medical officer about that and, of course,

the driver who actually brought the coach home, but I have known cases . . .'

'This idea that Noone picked up an acquaintance could only mean that he picked up another coach-driver, don't you think? We may be able to get a line on that. It shouldn't be too difficult to find out which other coaches were at the Hall at the approximate time that day.'

'It need not necessarily have been somebody who was in charge of a coach, of course.'

'I suppose not, and that doesn't help these needle-in-a-haystack goings-on. What made you mention the soil was found in Noone's hair? They'd have had to dump the body somewhere while daylight lasted.'

'It might be worth-while to find out whether there was any trace in a half-dug grave in the churchyard at that date. A grave was in process of being dug when I visited the churchyard and I noticed two others which had been filled in but looked new.'

'They'd have been spotted dumping the body. You only said "murderer".'

'Oh, there must have been two of them, as you say. Anyway, the body had to be disposed of quickly and in a place they could find very easily after dark. They had only to watch their opportunity. Of course, there may be nothing in this theory of mine unless somebody in the village saw something suspicious.'

'I doubt it. We've combed the neighbourhood pretty thoroughly and I doubt very much whether there is anything more to be learned around Hulliwell village.'

CHAPTER 7

The Watchman Waketh But In Vain

'If Daigh also is dead and his body hidden in a similar sort of place in Swansea,' said Laura, 'the murderer might take the hint and shift it somewhere else, don't you think?'

'Perhaps so, but I am not thinking of trying first in Swansea. There is the gatehouse of the bishop's palace at Dantwylch which must be explored, I think,' said Dame Beatrice. 'The coach went to Swansea, it is true, but I doubt whether a body went in it. The object of the murderer would have been to get rid of the evidence as soon as he possibly could. To transport it from Dantwylch to the docks at Swansea would have been to take an incalculable risk, because anything might have happened on the journey – engine failure involving attendance at a garage, an accident on the road, a police trap . . .'

'Our engines don't fail. The other things are possibilities, no doubt. Where do you think Noone's death took place?' asked Honfleur.

'Well, certainly not on top of that gatehouse.'

'Because the police did not find traces of blood on the roof at Hulliwell?'

'No, but because I think he was killed in the coach.' She repeated what she had said to the Chief Constable,

'But surely there would have been bloodstains on the floor or on one of the seats?' suggested Honfleur.

'No. A wound of that nature could have bled internally only. I have known of such cases. The weapon, as visualised by the doctors who examined Noone's body, must have been a very sharp-pointed knife with a six-or seven-inch blade. It penetrated deep into the heart and there could have been really no evidence of external bleeding, particularly if the weapon was left sticking in the body for a bit. When I looked in at the churchyard in Hulliwell village, the sexton and his assistant were digging a grave, and I noticed that there were two other graves fairly recently filled in. One of them, before the burial of its rightful occupant took place, could have made a convenient dumping-place for Noone's body as soon as dusk fell, and then the murderers could have returned for it in the dead hours of the night and . . .'

'Murderers? More than one?'

'I think so, because of the difficulty of getting the corpse on to the roof of the gatehouse. One would have climbed the ladder first and then, when the second — a stronger man — hoisted the body up the ladder, there would be a hand at the top to help with pulling the body on to the roof. Even so, it could not have been an easy task, because the corpse would have stiffened, most likely, by then.'

'But if he was killed in the coach, where did they hide the body before dusk fell and they could risk dumping it in the open grave?'

'In the boot of the coach, of course. At Hulliwell Hall the boot was empty. All the luggage was at the hotel. A boot capable of taking thirty persons' luggage could certainly have taken a corpse.'

'Then the body went back to the Dovedale hotel.'

'And was transferred to a fast car, no doubt, while the coach-party was at dinner.'

'It was taking an awful risk. Suppose, in broad daylight, somebody had come by while the body was being carried out of the inside of the coach and bundled into the boot?' asked Laura.

'They, or he, for I believe this part of the business could have been done by one man, had only to drive the coach on to the moors and watch for his opportunity.'

'I wonder he did not dump the body there on the moor and leave the.police to find it.'

'The plan was that neither body was to be found for a very considerable time – time for the murderers to leave the country, I imagine. It would have been very difficult to trace them after months, perhaps years, had gone by.'

'Wasn't it a bit elaborate, this business of first dumping the body in an open grave and then hoisting it on top of the gatehouse?' said Honfleur.

'Two minds were at work. One man was in favour of your suggestion, to dump the body and leave the police to find it. The other wanted it hidden to gain time.'

'Do you think they've already gone abroad?'

'It depends upon whether their business here is concluded. Well, I shall go back to Dantwylch to find out, if I can, what has happened to Daigh. The discovery of Noone's body has been a break-through, of course, but I am sorry it could not have been kept out of the newspapers. The murderers will have been warned and anything may happen now. My hope is that they will panic and so make at least one bad mistake.'

'So long as the mistake is not to kill another of my drivers! As it happens, the man on sick leave has reported back for duty, so that relieves us a bit. He is on the Skye run, so I do hope he really is feeling fit. I don't want him having to go sick again, both for his sake and my own. This business of finding Noone's murdered body, coupled with the disappearance of Daigh and the hijacking of his coach, hasn't done the general morale at our depot the least bit of good, I can tell you. If it gets any lower I may have to take a coach out myself, just to show the flag, as it were.'

'Could you not use Signor Vittorio?' asked Dame Beatrice flippantly. 'He can drive a car.'

'Oh, I passed up on Vittorio months ago. I began to wonder

what he was up to and how he got hold of some of the bits he tried to flog to me. Then, when you tipped me off about that Chinese stuff which he had shown Miss Mendel and had tried to sell me, I thought it was high time to sever the connection. I was tactful, of course. Told him that now the Welsh dresser, which I'd found for myself, was completely stocked, I'd lost interest and was thinking of going over to France and handling the Continental side of our business myself and expanding it. I *have* turned that idea over in my mind, as a matter of fact. There might be big opportunities if we could run our Continental tours from over there instead of from here. We might do Greece and Turkey, as well as the south of Italy, none of which we touch at present.'

'I see. And how did Vittorio receive this information?'

'Shrugged his shoulders, wished me luck and said that he had much enjoyed our acquaintanceship. Whether he put two and two together and realised that I thought some of his acquisitions might come from rather dubious sources, of course I don't know, but we parted amicably enough. I hope he *did* take the hint. He did his best to find me the things I wanted, and he was an amusing sort of chap in his way.'

' "The Smiler With the Knife," ' quoted Dame Beatrice absently. Honfleur looked startled.

'You don't mean that?' he cried.

'Mean what? Oh, good gracious me! Does one ever learn to cope with the subconscious mind when, occasionally, it chooses to rear its ugly head?'

'Oh, that's all right, then,' said Honfleur, relieved. 'I knew you must be joking.'

Dame Beatrice did not reply to this. She changed the subject to her proposed second journey into Wales, but later, to Laura, she said, 'There's many a true word spoken in jest, and this would fit. How beautifully, how logically, how perhaps all too easily it would fit! But it is useless and wrong to jump to conclusions at this stage of the enquiry. I must keep an open mind.'

For some reason, perhaps again there was more prompting from the subconscious, Dame Beatrice found that she was not particularly surprised by the next development. She had made all her preparations for departure, and Laura was actually seated at the wheel of the car, when Honfleur's call came through. A third coach-driver had disappeared, this time on the tour to West Scotland and Skye.

'Can you possibly call and see me?' asked the worried man.

'I am about to depart for Wales, but I could break my journey,' she replied.

'I do so wish you would. At my office, not my house, if you don't object. I've got to be here now this wretched news has come in. I only heard it half an hour ago and I'm nearly out of my mind. There won't be a man willing to take a coach anywhere after this! Thank goodness we're getting near the end of the season!'

'Well,' said Dame Beatrice, when she met him, 'this is a pretty state of affairs, is it not? And there is disaffection among your men?'

'Not yet, but there will be when they know about this third disappearance. At the moment every coach is on the road. We go out on Mondays, Saturdays and Sundays, you see, so at mid-week every driver is taking out a tour. The nine-day trips go on Saturdays and the six-day and seven-day on Mondays or Sundays. The idea is that, whichever tour is taken, the passengers are never back later than the following Sunday evening, so that they can get to work, if necessary, on the Monday morning after their tour ends. Some companies do ten- to fourteen-day tours, but we don't, except on the Continent. That's one reason why I'd like to get out there. If we could shorten up a twelve- or thirteen-day tour to nine days, we could run more often and also I believe we'd get extra bookings. At present our Continental coaches are rarely fully booked, and that's uneconomic.'

He appeared to be about to expand on the subject, but Dame

Beatrice checked the flow with a direct question.

'So when I have been to Wales, would you like me to visit Scotland?'

'Why not leave Wales to the police and go straight to Fort William? The trail up there will still be hot.'

'Are you more concerned about this man than about the second driver?'

'No, no, of course not, but I suppose I've got a special feeling for him I was entirely responsible for getting him a job here. He wasn't seconded to us from the buses, as most of our fellows are, but he was down on his luck after the war and came and asked me if I'd got anything for him. He'd been a van driver, but got into trouble for stealing cigarettes. The company didn't press charges, but they sacked him. He asked me to give him a chance. I was dubious, needless to say, but he was frank with me about his record and I knew it was his first lapse, and I took a bet with myself that it would be his last. I knew the man, you see, because he'd been in my unit during the war. He was a first-class soldier. Didn't mind what risks he ran. Brave as a lion. He said he'd yielded to a sudden temptation and I believed him.'

'I see.'

'And now this has to happen to him!'

'You must be an extremely worried man.'

'Honestly, Dame Beatrice, this third disappearance has knocked me endwise. One thing: the police really *will* have to charge into the matter bald-headed now.'

'The police are doing that already, since they know a driver has been murdered. What happened, so far as you have been told, in the case of this third driver? Did he also disappear on a day's outing after the passengers had left the coach to go sight-seeing?'

'No. He *does* appear to have vanished from the hotel itself. It's in a fairly remote sort of spot right down on the shore of the loch with nothing but a narrow road between it and the water. The coach did the Skye trip and Knight, the driver, had dinner with the passengers, but in the morning there was the coach still parked at the back of the hotel, but with no sign of the driver. The passengers' baggage was neatly stacked in the hotel vestibule, where the hotel porters had put it, but the driver's bed was untouched and the passengers have not seen him again.'

'So what steps were taken?'

'Fortunately we've got a man in Edinburgh whom the Scottish hotels are asked to contact if anything untoward happens. He 'phoned me this morning to tell me what steps he had taken.'

'So you are prepared for emergencies?'

'It is in case of a road accident or the driver or one of the passengers being taken ill. Well, the Edinburgh chap got the Scottish Tourist Board on the job and they sent a coach to collect our passengers and take them to their hotel in Perth. Meanwhile we shall have to take another driver up by car to the hotel at Saighdearan to collect our own coach, drive it to Perth and bring our passengers home. There's been no more sign of Knight than there was of the other two drivers and we're particularly anxious about him because he had been on sick leave, as I said, for some time, and only came back to take this Scottish tour out of loyalty to us because he knew how short-handed we were after losing Noone and Daigh.'

'So we go to Scotland,' said Laura, pleased.

'After we have visited Dantwylch again,' amended Dame Beatrice.

The Cathedral Close at Dantwylch was walled around like a city and much of the stone walls was still standing. Originally there had been four fortified entrance-gates, for the mediaeval bishops either mistrusted or did not rely upon the hill-top castle which had been built to protect them. The gatehouse to the palace itself, which Laura had found walled off from the ruined chapel, had been an extra defence, but not the only one.

The way by which visitors now approached the Cathedral and the ruins had been one of the original ways down into the dip in the hills where the buildings were situated, but the path had lost its gatehouse and was now no more than a gap in the walls from which the public descended, by means of a long flight of steps and a steep slope, to reach the West Door of the Cathedral.

Opposite the West Door a further path ended in the narrow bridge crossed by Laura and Dame Beatrice on their previous visit, and beyond the bridge a rougher path led to the gatehouse.

Dame Beatrice attached little importance to the police inspection of its roof. Had some of the former entrances to the palace courtyard been open to the public, she might have had hopes of its gatehouse, but, except for one which led only to the archdeacon's house, which was almost on the perimeter of the Cathedral Close, there was no entrance wide enough to take a car or a motor-coach or anything else in which a body could have been transported unseen.

The gatehouse which gave access to the archdeacon's lodging was in poor repair, but was still standing and was only about twenty yards from the town highway. Thus it was a likelier hiding-place than the archbishop's ruins. However, it offered no admission to the public and was firmly labelled PRIVATE.

'I imagine that the archdeacon would be glad to have a body removed from the top of his gatehouse if, indeed, a body is there,' said Dame Beatrice, gazing from the approach road and through the archdeacon's iron gates at the crude and partly ruinous little structure.

'No doubt, lady *bach*,' agreed the Welsh inspector of police, 'and we shall leave no stone unturned. Thorough we are, here in Dantwylch. There is another gatehouse to be inspected before we trouble the archdeacon.'

'The gatehouse which is still standing at the entrance to the ruins of the bishop's palace?' said Dame Beatrice. 'Yes, but it would have been a dangerous and difficult proceeding to carry a body so great a distance from the road. It is not as though a vehicle could have been used.'

'All those steps, you mean. True that is, then, but we will take a look, all the same, just to make sure. My men will be along with an aluminium ladder.'

His men trundled the extending ladder on a two-wheeled truck down the public steps and the subsequent incline and then across the bridge which spanned the stream. There was nobody about, as it happened, to see the sergeant climb to the top of the gatehouse. To nobody's surprise, his activities had no result.

'Never mind, boyo,' said the inspector. 'You did your best. Thorough we are, see?'

'All right with the archdeacon, then?' asked the sergeant, adding a belated 'sir' as an afterthought.

'All right with the archdeacon, boyo,' the inspector responded, 'though a surprise for him, of course, to think of a body on his property, perhaps. Nothing here, then? No surprise about that. We will now take the short cut past the Cathedral, look you, and follow the archdeacon's little private path up the hill. The entrance to the old tower – nearly in ruins it is, but strong enough still, I am told – is on the side away from the town, on the inside of the gateway.'

With the two constables pushing the light trolley with the ladder and the cortège reinforced by Laura, who had been taking another look at the remains of the bishop's palace, they made their way to their objective.

The archdeacon's gatehouse was an ugly, clumsy little building consisting of one octagonal and one round tower bridged by what had been the watchman's room. A low, narrow doorway in the octagonal tower proved to be the only obvious means of entrance, but the door itself was locked. The inspector produced the key which had been supplied at the archdeacon's residence. It was a heavy iron affair about seven inches long.

'I think, if you don't mind,' the inspector said, as he inserted it, 'I will take first look, just in case, you know. Do not wish to upset ladies by seeing dead men, do we, then?'

The others waited below while he mounted a stair so narrow

that he could scarcely thrust his broad shoulders between the walls. They could hear him stumbling on the newel treads. Even from where they stood they were aware of a horrible, sweetish odour which came wafting down into the open air. Automatically they moved back from the doorway.

The inspector came down immediately, blew his nose vigorously and then gulped in some deep breaths of the mild, fresh air which came in over Ramsay Sound.

'He is there, oh, yes, indeed,' he said. He stepped well back from the tower and then, accompanied by Dame Beatrice, who was followed by Laura, he went out to the archdeacon's gate to look up at the building from the side which faced the approach-road from the town.

The octagonal tower had windows on three of its faces. These had been boarded up. The porter's room, which formed the connection between it and the lesser round tower, also had windows, but only one of these was obscured. The other was open to the air and was not more than ten feet from the ground.

The inspector called to his sergeant and pointed to the aperture.

'Bring the ladder,' he said. 'We shall need to carry him down through the window. Did you bring a sheet with you, then? And the ambulance waiting? Is lovely!' He turned to Dame Beatrice. 'Thorough we are, look you, in Dantwylch. Oh, yes, and now so clever you are, lady *bach*, something more I can tell you. We found out which man was on duty, see, when that coach left the car-park and was found at Swansea. Jones the Ticket told us he was surprised at the card the coach-driver handed in. 'Why, man,' he says, 'you have only been here a matter of ten minutes.' The driver says, 'One of my passengers was taken bad, see? Got to get him to hospital.' Then Jones the Ticket sees somebody stretched out on the floor of the coach and a waterproof spread over him and his face covered. Well, I now think it was not a sick man, but a dead man that Jones saw on the floor of the coach, and I think it was *this* dead man, look you.'

CHAPTER 8

The Hotel on Loch Linnhe

'But Scotland isn't England,' protested Basil Honfleur, demonstrating yet again the English genius for understatement, 'so I do wish you'd go up there, even now, and find out what's happened to poor Knight.'

'I can do nothing that the police cannot do much better, now that two bodies have been found.'

'Oh, come, now, dash it! The police would never have found those two bodies if it hadn't been for you.'

'Laura, not I. But, even so, it was only a question of time. The police would have found them sooner or later.'

'Anyway, this time we shall be quicker off the mark. Knight only disappeared four days ago. Surely the sooner we get on the trail the better?'

'The same applies to the police and, unlike myself, they are on the trail already. The fact that now they know your drivers not only disappeared but have been murdered will add much more zest to their efforts than may have been their initial urge when they thought that they were chasing merely a couple of runaways. They *really* have something to go on this time. By the way, was Knight your regular driver on that tour?'

'No. He offered to do a stint to help us out and that was the tour without a driver.'

'I see.'

'You mean you won't go up there, then, and look into things for yourself and on our behalf?'

'For myself, well, yes. Curiosity, apart from my dislike of murder, will impel me to continue my investigations.'

'My Company will be glad to . . .'

'I am not interested in rewards and I do not believe in fairies.'

'But we'd *like* to express . . .'

'Look, my dear Mr Honfleur, does not one thing strike you very forcibly?'

'How do you mean?'

'If you have not guessed my meaning it will be kinder if I do not expound it.'

Basil Honfleur got up from his chair and walked to the window of his office. The view was pleasant. The window did not overlook the busy bus station but gave a prospect of the municipal park. There were lawns, trees and flower-beds and among these meandered a tiny stream. Broad paths were thronged with holiday crowds, but their laughter and conversation scarcely penetrated to the room, which was high up in the building. Faintly, also, like the dying fall referred to by Shakespeare, came the far-off music played by the municipal orchestra, for the bandstand was opposite the window from which Honfleur surveyed the scene.

He remained where he was for a minute or two and then turned to Dame Beatrice.

'I won't pretend I don't understand you,' he said. 'You mean this dreadful business is something to do with our organisation, don't you?'

'I think that, somewhere among your members, you have what my secretary would call a bent operator.'

'Yes,' said Honfleur gloomily, 'I know all the evidence suggests that, particularly the hi-jacking of the coach in Wales and the planting of it in Swansea. But it doesn't follow, you know. Our chaps are by no means the only people who can handle a coach. Take that tank chap at Hulliwell, for example. If he could take that coach-load back to their hotel without any trouble, so could hundreds of others.'

'That is true. Where is the passenger list for this tour conducted by Knight?'

'As we live there, we picked up the coach in Canonbury,' said Mrs Grant. 'I travelled with my neighbour, Mrs Kingsbury, while our husbands went fishing. I did a coach tour with Ian last year. I liked it, but he was less keen. Anyway, we agreed that it wasn't a bad idea to have separate holidays for a change, so he fixed up with Edward Kingsbury while I went off with Susan. We took a room with twin beds because we thought you got a better room that way, and we know each other quite well, so neither of us minded sharing and it's more companionable, too.

'We stayed the first night in Harrogate and went on to Edinburgh. We had thought of going out after dinner, but it rained. It was still raining when we left at nine on the following morning — Monday, that would have been — but the rain cleared away before lunch, so we had a really enjoyable run, although it was too misty to see much at first.

'We crossed the Forth Bridge and had a rather poor coffee-stop, I thought. It was only so that people could use the loo, of course. I don't think anybody bothered with coffee; it wasn't that sort of place. But the lunch stop was delightful, right at the end of Loch Earn, and we had enough time to walk around a little, when the meal was over, and look at the view. The driver came with Susan and me and told us the names of the mountains, but, of course, I don't remember what they were.'

'The driver? Mr Knight?'

'Yes. Such a helpful man and so knowledgeable. There wasn't a question he couldn't answer, although he said he had done the tour only once before.'

'So you had no suspicions?'

'Suspicions of what?'

'That he might have had something on his mind, perhaps.'

'Good heavens, no, except that I suppose the drivers must always have something on their minds. It must be a big responsibility to have thirty people depending on you for nine whole days and all that driving to do. He was always most jovial, though. When we got back on to the coach after the next stop, which was for tea after we'd been through Glen Coe, he said, 'You think you're going to Fort William, don't you? Well, you're not.' I remember I felt very disappointed. I wondered whether that meant we were not going to Skye, either, because, of course, they reserve the right to change the route, but, as it turned out, all was well. We stayed at a new hotel, most of it built bungalow-fashion with one three-storey wing, and, I must say, it was excellent. It was about five miles south of Fort William and —'

'Ah, yes,' said Dame Beatrice, who did not want to waste time in listening to a description of a hotel which she herself proposed to visit in the near future, 'and it was from that hotel that Knight disappeared.'

'He sat at dinner the first night with Susan and me and a man who had come on his own, and Knight was as cheerful and talkative as ever. After dinner Susan and I went for a stroll. The hotel was on the shores of Loch Linnhe and it was a lovely evening. There were mountains on the other side of the loch and the water was calm and lovely. If Ian had been there instead of Susan it would have been like our honeymoon. (We spent it in the Highlands.) When we got back, the woman who sat behind us in the coach was reading people's palms and there was a big group round her, of course, and a lot of laughing and exclamations. The tour had certainly got into its stride and everybody seemed relaxed and happy, especially Mr Knight. I suppose it's a relief to know a tour is going well.'

'And on the following day you went to Skye.'

'Yes, but the best part of the drive was from Fort William to Kyle of Lochalsh. *That* was glorious, especially after we turned westwards at Invergarry. Skye wasn't nearly so impressive, but I don't think we saw the best part of it, because we took the road straight up to Portree on the east side and didn't get any real views of the Cuillins or anything like that.'

'And after you got back from Skye?'

'I think most people turned in fairly early. I wrote some post-cards and then Susan and I went to bed. We talked about the views of Ben Nevis we had seen on the way back.'

'Did you see any more of the driver after he had brought the party back from Skye?'

'Oh, yes. Somebody bought him a drink at the bar and he was at dinner – not with us, of course, this time. He had to go the rounds. After dinner he was not in the lounge for coffee and I concluded he was checking the coach against the next day's run.'

'And you never saw him again?'

'No. He wasn't at breakfast, but nobody thought anything about that, because we concluded he'd had his early so as to get all our suitcases on board ready for the nine o'clock start, but when we came out from breakfast and Susan had been back to our room to make sure the suitcases had been collected from outside the bedroom door and that we'd left nothing behind, we went to the hotel reception to hand in our key and there was all the luggage still stacked in the vestibule and no sign of Knight or the coach. One of the porters was asking whether anyone had seen him, but, of course, nobody had.'

'But the coach was still there? He had not gone off in it?'

'Oh, no, it was where, I suppose, he had parked it overnight behind the hotel. Well, we hung about and hung about. Some sat in the lounge, others looked at the things in the hotel shop, then the newspapers came in, so that helped a bit. I spoke to the manager, but he couldn't tell us a thing except that Mr Knight must have thumbed a lift into Fort William to buy something and hadn't been able to get a lift back.'

'Was Knight's room searched?'

'Oh, yes, when he didn't turn up, and that was the queerest

thing of all. One or two of our men went along with the
chambermaid to find out whether he'd been taken ill, but the
room was empty and his bed was untouched.'

'What about his suitcase?'

'His suitcase? I've no idea. Nobody mentioned that, and it
didn't occur to me to ask. Well, in the end, another driver turned
up — I suppose the hotel manager telephoned for him. He came
from Edinburgh. We were taken to Perth, which was our next
overnight stop, but there was no coffee-break and a very late
lunch that day, and everybody was wondering what had
happened to Mr Knight. There were some nasty rumours
because, of course, most people had read about the other driver.'

Dame Beatrice did not mention that the last word could now
be put in the plural. All she said was:

"And that was the end of the matter, so far as you were concerned?'

'Well, yes. I mean, there was nothing we could do, was there?
We got home all right, because they sent another driver up from
County Coaches for us, but it wasn't the same happy party. The
driver was a very taciturn man and, anyway, losing Mr Knight
like that quite spoilt the holiday, although, of course, it did give
us something to talk about for the rest of the trip.'

'Oh, yes? What sort of things were mentioned?'

'Well, as I said, people remembered that, about a month
before, another driver had disappeared and had been found
murdered in Derbyshire. I knew nothing about that at the time,
because Ian and I had been visiting our married daughter in
Spain, where she and her husband had rented a flat for a month,
and we didn't get the English papers there, but there was a lot of
talk after we got back, apart from all the gossip on the coach.'

'I see.' Dame Beatrice still did not reveal that another driver
had been found murdered, this time in Wales, for that bit of
news had not been leaked to the press and so was not public
property. 'The two cases are not analogous, though.'

'Not?'

'No. In the Derbyshire affair the driver disappeared at midday while his passengers were inspecting a stately home.'

'I don't see that it makes any difference.'

'And his coach had been moved a few yards from the spot on which he left it. Of course, it may have been moved merely to accommodate another vehicle. I wonder whether your coach had been moved during the night?'

'I wouldn't know.'

'Perhaps the people at the hotel can tell me.'

'Oh, you are going up there?'

'As I am being retained by the Company to watch their interests, I think I should see the conditions for myself. By the way, Mrs Grant, did Driver Knight make any mention of the fact that he had returned recently from sick leave?'

'Not so far as I know. He must have made a good recovery. I never saw a healthier-looking man.'

The hamlet – although it was scarcely large enough to merit even that description – was called Saighdearan. Apart from the hotel, it consisted of an ugly, raw-looking motel a couple of hundred yards further along the road to Fort William, a lorry-drivers' café and half-a-dozen cottages put up by a speculative builder for holiday letting. There were also a couple of owner-occupied bungalows on a slope above the hotel and there was a large house further along the loch-side, but it had fallen into ruins and was unoccupied.

A busy road ran between the hotel and the steep-sided banks of the loch. There was a grey, stony shore, muddy and uninviting, but on the further side the mountains were reflected in the water and the reflections were calm, clear and beautiful.

Laura had booked in by telephone and as soon as they had tidied up after the drive from Carlisle, where they had spent the night, Dame Beatrice made no secret of her errand to the hotel manager, a massive, bearded man wearing a tweed jacket and a beautiful kilt in the tartan of MacDonald of Clanranald.

'That?' he said. 'Yes, a very strange business, to be sure. So you are here on behalf of County Tours, whose driver he was. Well, there's little I can tell you. The police have all the information I can give.'

'I am wondering whether you have any theories which perhaps you have not imparted to the police.'

'No, no, I am not one to indulge in speculation. From what I heard, this is not the first case of its kind.'

'That is what makes it so serious.'

'Aye, right enough. Well, I'll recapitulate for your benefit, but there's nothing I can tell you that you will not know already.'

He proceeded to give an account which tallied in all respects with that which she had had already from Mrs Grant, except that the missing man's suitcase, neatly packed, was still in the hotel.

'I suppose Knight did not have any visitors from outside while the party was here?' she asked. 'I note that your lounge bar and your dining-room are open to non-residents.'

'He had no visitors. The coach arrived on the first evening at six, dinner was at seven and he sat at table with three of the passengers. On the following morning the coach left at nine to go over to Skye and he dined that night with some of the other passengers. I always take a look round the dining-room to make sure all is well and everybody is happy, so I am sure he was there. He appeared to be making himself very agreeable to the ladies, as was his custom.'

'And that, I assume, is the last you saw of him. I understand he did not take coffee that evening.'

'Aye, that's true.'

'You did not see him go to his room?'

'Nobody saw him. He would likely have taken the covered way from the dining-room without going through the lounge.'

'I suppose you did not hear a car come into your front parking-space that night? The space you keep for casual visitors?'

'There would be cars coming and going up to the end of the licensing hours, of course, and, far into the night, there would be cars going by on the road.'

'Oh, of course. How many exits are there to the hotel?'

'There will be four, including the one from the hotel shop. There is another at the hotel entrance by the reception desk, another opposite the shop on the corridor which leads to the ground-floor bedrooms, and one more at the foot of the stairs up to the three-storey wing where Knight had his room. He could have slipped away easily enough without anybody being the wiser, so long as he bided his time and watched that nobody was about, but why should he want to slip away? He wasn't owing me money.'

'So there doesn't seem to be a lead anywhere,' said Laura, when they were discussing the affair in Dame Beatrice's room after dinner that evening. 'What's the next move? Do we look for another dead body, do you suppose? I'm getting morbid about this business.'

'The manager has consented to my questioning the hotel staff, although he assures me – and I have a feeling he is right – that they can tell me nothing which they have not already told the police.'

'Is it worth while to bother them, then?'

'I think, for my own satisfaction, it must be done.'

'I could do a bit of rubber-necking round the village, if that would be of any help. You'd have to tell me what you want me to say, though.'

' "That shall be tomorrow, not tonight." '

' "I must bury sorrow out of sight," ' capped Laura, grinning. 'Browning could be as banal as Shakespeare when he liked, couldn't he?'

'Heresy of the deepest dye!'

'About Shakespeare? What price some of those ghastly rhyming couplets at the end of scenes in Macbeth, to name but one play?'

'Curtain lines on an uncurtained stage? I am not well-informed on the subject of the Elizabethan theatre.'

'Be that as it may, I'll say good-night, then, before I become tediously informative. What time breakfast?'

'Half-past eight, I think.'

'Right. I wonder whether there would be any joy in having a swim in the loch? It ain't the plunging-in I mind; it's the perishing getting-out.'

For what it might turn out to be worth, there was one scrap of information which, after breakfast on the following morning, Dame Beatrice gleaned from a previously untapped source. This was a boy of sixteen who had not been questioned by the police for the simple reason that he had not been in the hotel at the time of their visit.

It was Laura who discovered him and obtained an item of information while Dame Beatrice was interviewing the chambermaids.

'You'd better talk to him, I think,' she said to her employer. 'He says he was "away to Oban" when the police called, but he did encounter a stranger whom he describes as "a black man". That, in these parts, could mean anybody darkish – a Spaniard or a Pakistani – let alone a Sudanese the colour of a black boot.'

'What is the youth's name?'

'Wullie MacKay.'

'And where shall I find him?'

'In the yard behind the scullery. He's gutting the fish we're to have for lunch. The hotel buys in bulk from the quayside and the eviscerations are one of Wullie's jobs. He seems to be a man-of-all-work.'

Dame Beatrice opened the conversation with the lad by asking how the name of the hamlet ought to be pronounced. She gave her own phonetic rendering of Saighdearan.

'Och, no!' said Wullie, far too polite to show amusement. He pronounced it for her.

'Ah! Sy-tshir-un!' echoed Dame Beatrice. 'I am obliged to

you. Would it have a meaning in English?'

'Aye. Saighdearan will be meaning Soldiers.'

'Indeed? It ties up with Fort William, I suppose?'

'That place,' said Wullie darkly, 'will be having another name put upon it when we get our way.'

'You are a Scottish Nationalist, are you? But surely your own name is William? Besides, what about William Wallace? He was also a great nationalist, although, I believe, by birth a Welshman.'

Wullie threw away the entrails of the fish he was cleaning and they were swooped upon by a squawking, hostile bird. He said,

I'll no play with words. What would it be that you are wanting with myself?'

'A description of the black man.'

'Och, him!' said Wullie, evincing no surprise. 'He was a little, thin fellow, maybe like a tinker, but I think he was a foreign man. Besides, he had money. He was showing me an English five-pound note and saying it would be for myself if I would tell him which coach-party was staying here and what would be the name of the driver.'

'And could you tell him that?'

'Och, aye.'

'And he gave you the five pounds?'

'That, no.'

'Why ever not?'

'I kenned he was up to no good, so I was telling him the wrong party and the wrong driver. He said that was no' what he was after and he ganged away and took the five pounds with him.'

'Did you ever see him again?'

'I did not.' He threw a fish-head to a passing cat and bent all his attention on his work.

'Well, it is a pity that you should be done out of five pounds because of scruples which become you,' said Dame Beatrice, producing an equivalent bank-note and laying it on the end of the wooden block on which he was so sedulously operating. 'Would you care to comment on an idea which I entertain? I think your black man was an Italian.'

'Keep your money, lady. I couldna say what his nationality might ha' been,' said Wullie, pointedly ignoring the gift. 'He was no' from these parts, anyway, and I didna trust him.'

Dame Beatrice left the five-pound note where it lay and went back to Laura.

'I tried another long shot,' she said, 'but it did not even leave the bowstring. Our next approach must be to the local inhabitants, as you suggested.'

'There can't be many of those. I've talked to the manager and, except for the people who run the motel and the restaurant and that scruffy good-pull-up-for-carmen along the road, the only birds who are more or less resident, he tells me, are a man called Carstairs and the Whites.'

'And these are?'

'The people in those villa residences up on the slope behind us. Carstairs is an artist and a bird of passage. White is a chap who runs a boat-hire business in Fort William.'

'Let us have speech with these local inhabitants, then.'

'Do we put our cards on the table?'

'If you think that would be the best approach. I shall leave Mr Carstairs and the Whites to you while I tackle the motel and the holiday cottages. The lorrydrivers' café can come later.'

'If we get no joy from the other places, you mean. Right. How would it be if I represented myself as Knight's sorrowing sister, all bemused and bothered by his mysterious disappearance? I'll get as close a description of him as I can from the people here, and then I'll put on a Niobe act, shall I?'

'Niobe wept for her children, not for her brother Pelops.'

'I bet Carstairs and the Whites won't bother about that. Anyway, there can't be anything much to do here except watch the comings and goings at the hotel. I don't wonder Carstairs is migratory. Greatly as I love my native land, I don't think I could stick it in a place like this all the year round. It must be miserably dull for Mrs White. Carstairs, I'm told, is a bachelor and more often away than not, so he's all right, I suppose, and White has his business in Fort William. Wonder whether Mrs White will talk to me? I daresay she will be glad of a good gossip.'

'You had all this from the manager here?'

'Yes, and from some of the maids.'

'I suppose you did not find out what was in the suitcase which Knight left in his room?'

'Yes, I did ask, as a matter of fact. There were his pyjamas, a light dressing-gown, his washing materials and a good navy-blue suit which the manager says he put on in the evenings.'

'No spare underwear?'

'Oh, yes, of course. A clean shirt and a pair of briefs, but that is the sum total.'

'So, wherever he went –'

'Looks as though he meant to come back, doesn't it? I think we're looking for another body.'

'There could be other explanations, but that seems the likeliest at present.'

CHAPTER 9

Saighdearan, Place of Soldiers

White's middle name was MacGregor. Laura learned this when she called at the bungalow. A woman answered the door.

'Mr *MacGregor* White?' she asked, when Laura enquired for him.

'Well, yes, if it isn't Mr Lamont White,' said Laura, who had taken an instant dislike to the woman, who, from her accent, was English. 'The Whites are almost bound to be one or the other, aren't they?'

'I wouldn't know. I happen to be English.'

'I wonder whether you can help me? I am trying to find out what has happened to the driver of a County Tours coach which pulled up at the hotel here a few days ago.'

'Are you from the police? I have already answered their questions.'

'I am connected with the Home Office and we have been authorised to make our own enquiries.'

'The Home Office?'

Laura produced one of Dame Beatrice's official cards.

'This is my employer,' she said. The woman read the card and opened the door wider.

'You'd better come in,' she said, 'although there is absolutely nothing I can tell you. I saw the coach you mean. It came in at about six in the evening and went off again next morning – to

101

Skye, my maid tells me. Then it returned. That is all I know.'

'You could see the coach from your windows?'

'Come and look for yourself. Not that I have time to spare looking out of windows, I assure you.'

There was a coach belonging to another tours company standing in the yard of the hotel. Laura had had a steep climb up a lane to reach the bungalow from the hotel, so the coach looked to be a long way below her and her main view was of its roof. It would be quite possible to see people getting in and out of it, she thought, but not so easy, perhaps, to give a clear description of them.

'You have heard about the death of another driver who worked for the County Tours people, I expect,' said Laura.

'Not until the police came here. I do not bother with the papers and my husband never discusses the news with me.'

'And nobody but the police came to your house to make enquiries?'

'Well, not the kind of enquiries you mean. Besides, it was my husband's business, not mine.'

'About the hire of a boat?'

'What else? Boat-hire is my husband's livelihood.'

'When was this?'

'It can have nothing to do with this missing man.'

'You mean he wasn't the person who made the enquiry?'

'Of course not. The only boat a coach-driver would be interested in is the ferry from Mallaig or Kyle of Lochalsh over to Skye. My husband lets out motor-boats and small yachts, or takes parties down the loch or across to Mull.'

'So, if it wasn't the driver, who was it? I assume that people usually hire from Fort William, not from this house.'

'I have no idea who it was, but you are wrong in supposing that people do not hire from this house. We have an understanding with Mr MacDonald at the hotel. He takes a small percentage when he recommends any of the hotel guests to my husband.'

'Oh, yes, of course. Do you know whether this particular man came from the hotel?'

'No, he didn't. He was staying at the motel down the road, or so he said.'

'Can you describe him to me?'

'No, that I can't. I didn't see him. My husband mentioned him, that's all.'

'For any special reason?'

'No, except that he said we did not often get enquiries for boats from the motel.'

'Their clients being birds of passage, I suppose. Did your husband happen to mention whether the enquirer was an Englishman?'

'He said he thought he was a foreigner.'

'Your husband isn't at home, of course?'

'He is in his office down at the boatyard, as usual. This is near the end of our busy time of year.'

'Do you know whether this man did actually hire a boat?'

'I suppose he did. My husband didn't say. I took it for granted that he did.'

'Well, thank you very much, Mrs White.'

'I'll see you to the door. My maid is out shopping for me in Fort William this morning.'

Laura felt that Mrs White deserved some compensation for help which, however grudgingly, had at least been given and might be valuable, so she said:

'Perhaps you won't spread it about just yet — tell your husband, if you like, of course — but there has been a second murder. Another coach-driver belonging to the same company was found dead three or four days ago. That is why we are so concerned about this third driver and why my employer and I have been called in to make some enquiries. My employer is the psychiatric consultant to the Home Office and will be called to testify when we catch the murderer.'

'You don't mean he is this foreigner?'

'Nobody knows — yet.'

'Well!' said Mrs White. 'Well! To think we may have had a murderer in this very house!'

'Oh, we mustn't jump to conclusions, you know,' said Laura. 'All the same, I would very much like to speak to your husband and get a description of this foreigner. Can you tell me how to find his boatyard?'

'No need,' said Mrs White, now expansive, excited and genial. 'He'll be here for his lunch at half-past one. I'll tell him to expect you at half-past two. That will give you time to have your own lunch, won't it?'

Laura, feeling she had misjudged the woman, returned cock-a-hoop to the hotel and then, as she reached the entrance, she remembered that she had not interviewed Carstairs. She decided to remedy this omission forthwith, but discovered that she might have saved herself a second climb up the hill. There was a notice, kept in place by a large stone, lying on the outside sill. *No more until further notice,* it read.

'Bread or milk, no doubt,' said Laura to herself. 'Oh, well, lucky to get it delivered in a place this distance from the town. Wonder whether Carstairs went away before or after Knight and his coach got to the hotel?'

She joined Dame Beatrice for lunch and at half-past two they climbed up to the Whites' bungalow. Mrs White, all graciousness this time, admitted them and introduced her husband. MacGregor White was a plump, broad-featured man who looked as though he ought to be genial but who turned out to be taciturn and morose. No, he did not keep a register of those who hired his boats. He entered dates and payments, but not names. No, he did not remember a foreigner calling at the house on any particular day, but, if his wife said so, they could take her word for it. Yes, the police had questioned him about a missing coach-driver and little joy they had gained from it! During the summer months numbers of people hired boats and on the day in question he must have had several enquiries. He did not even answer all of them himself. His assistant might have taken some of the bookings. No, they could not speak to his assistant. It was so near the end of the season that he had laid him off, as usual, until the following summer.

'It's seasonal work, you'll understand,' he said, suddenly apologetic as he caught Dame Beatrice's sardonic eye.

'Well, where does he hang out when he's not with you?' asked Laura. Grudgingly White supplied this information. It turned out that the man, whose name was McFee, had a small shop in Portree on Skye.

'Anyone will tell you,' said Mrs White, shepherding Dame Beatrice and Laura to the door, 'where it is. I've never been there myself.'

'Portree?' said Laura, as they walked down the slope towards the hotel. 'That's where the coach-party went before Knight disappeared, isn't it? We might pick up something there, don't you think? We know the hotel where they lunched. This might turn out to be our lucky strike. Besides, it's a wonderful drive from here to Kyle of Lochalsh. Do we go first thing tomorrow morning? Too late for a jaunt like that today.'

There was a glimpse of Ben Nevis after the car had left Fort William on the following morning, but nothing like the magnificent view of it which they could obtain on their return journey, as Laura knew. They met holiday traffic on their way to Spean Bridge, but after that they were fortunate. The glorious road to Kyle of Lochalsh was almost free of traffic and there was only a short wait at the ferry before Laura drove on to the boat for the very short crossing to Kyleakin.

Once clear of the village, the road up to Portree was comparatively dull after the amazingly lovely scenery of the mainland. However, Skye itself exercised its own magic and Laura, taking the coast road, found herself singing as they passed through Sligachan and headed north for their destination.

The post office at Portree, seemed the obvious place in which
to make enquiries and here the information Laura asked for was
readily obtained. The town was small and compact, and, following the directions, she and Dame Beatrice experienced no
difficulty in finding McFee's shop.

It turned out to be, primarily, an ironmonger's, but there were
also picture postcards and small souvenirs of a kind likely to at-
tract tourists, besides a collection of very ornamental kilt-pins
and a *sgiàn dhu* in a glass case which immediately attracted
Laura's attention.

The shopkeeper — McFee's wife, the callers assumed — saw
her looking at it and told her that, according to legend, it had
belonged to one of Prince Charles Edward's followers who had
left it to a McFee when he crossed with the prince to Raasay.
She and Laura got into conversation and it was a short step
from this to a mention of the Fort William boatyard and
MacGregor White.

'My man will be back,' said Mrs McFee, 'to his dinner. Hae
ye supped?'

'Booked lunch at the hotel,' said Laura. 'Did your husband ever mention a foreigner who booked a boat from Mr
White's yard about a week ago?'

'What way would he be mentioning that?' Mrs McFee enquired.

'Because the police are after the man and we're hoping that
Mr McFee may be able to tell us where he went. I suppose he
returned the boat?'

'That's no business of mine.' The woman, who had been
friendliness itself up to this point, looked suspiciously at Laura.
'You'll be a police-woman?' she asked.

'No, but a man has been murdered and we are acting on
behalf of the tour company which employed him.'

'You're no' the police?'

'No, but we are working in close collaboration with them. Is
your husband likely to be long?'

'Och, no. It's gone noon. He'll be here soon enough. I'll get you a chair.'

'We'd rather look round the shop,' said Laura. Dame Beatrice, who had left them during the exchanges, came to the proprietress with a Highland brooch which, when she had paid for it, she pinned to the lapel of her tweed jacket. Laura also decided to make one or two small purchases and, as she was being given her change, a stocky man came into the shop and handed Mrs McFee a parcel.

'I got it from McLeod,' he said. 'It's a fush.'

'The ladies wish to speak with you, Jock.'

'Och, aye.' He did not seem in the least surprised. Laura took it that this was his accustomed reaction to any news, good or bad. She herself, however, was surprised by Dame Beatrice's question to him.

'Would you have any idea,' she said, 'how long Mr Carstairs has been away?'

'Carstairs?'

'And whether he is married?'

'Now how would I ken that?'

'Because you are a sociable, gregarious man who likes to get to know the neighbours. I think you lived in your employer's bungalow in Saighdearan while you were working down at Mr White's boatyard in Fort William. Mr White seems to be a taciturn, unfriendly man and his wife has, I would think, the English suburban determination to keep herself to herself, but you are from . . .'

'Kirkintilloch. Aye, White will be what I call a Black Highlander. You're right enough there. But you were speaking of Carstairs. He isna married – that is, I never saw a wife. He took on yon wee house in Saighdearan maybe two years ago and he runs a big green car, a Wolseley. I dinna ken what might be his business, but it was seldom he stayed in Saighdearan, so at my guess he travelled in some kind of goods, but he was not a man you could question.'

'We were told he was an artist.'

'Och, weel noo, he micht be juist that same.'

'Did he ever hire a boat?'

'No' to my knowledge.'

'Was he an Englishman?'

'Aye.'

'How long is it since you gave up your summer employment with Mr White?'

'Last Saturday.'

'Was Mr Carstairs at Saighdearan when you left?'

'He wisna, but he had been there, on and off, for the past year.'

'On and off?'

'Aye. Times he would be there, but most times not. But what way are you speiring at me wi' all this?'

'Because I represent the Home Office and am working with the police. We think Mr Carstairs may be able to help our enquiries into a case of murder – double murder.'

'Losh! Ye dinna say!'

'Is there anything else you can tell me about him?'

'I dinna ken. He was a pleasant enough wee man.'

'You mean he was a small man?'

'Five foot seven at the most, but awfu' strong in the arms and shoulders. He telt me once that his hobby was lifting weights, barbells, ye ken, and the like. Aye, and his press-ups! Ye'd think the man would drop dead of heart-failure.'

'Did you ever see him in conversation with a dark-skinned man, a foreigner?'

'No' to my recollection. It's little I saw of him at all.'

'Did you, by any chance, hire out a boat to a foreigner, possibly an Italian, recently?'

'A wee, wee man awfu' like a monkey? He spoke to White, no' to me. But it wisna for a boat. He had his own cruiser. It was about a fault in the engine, but White couldna help him.'

'Did you see the County Tours coach come in last week?'

'I did not. I was down at the boatyard with Mr White until eight o' the clock.'

'You know that, after the trip over here and after the coach-party had lunched at the hotel and looked at the shops, the coach-driver disappeared?'

'Aye, so I heard.'

'Did you set eyes on him at all before he went?'

'I did not. They would have been back from Skye before I left the boatyard and come the morn he was awa', or so it was telt me.'

Laura drove Dame Beatrice back to Saighdearan. The late afternoon turned misty and a penetrating rain began to fall, so that the windscreen wipers were busy all the way from Kyle of Lochalsh to Saighdearan and the views, including that of Ben Nevis, were lost in impenetrable haze.

Laura spoke little during the journey. For one thing, she needed all her concentration to look out for the headlights of on-coming cars and to keep her own vehicle safely on the road; for another, although she was burning with curiosity, she thought it better to ask no questions, although she felt sure that she knew in what direction Dame Beatrice's thoughts had travelled during the interview with McFee. Just as they left Fort William, however, Dame Beatrice spoke.

'So we have to find out whether Carstairs and Knight are one and the same man,' she said.

'Do you think that's likely?'

'I think it is most unlikely. Knight would hardly bring a coach to a place where he was already known as Carstairs.'

'It depends upon whether the manager of the hotel knows him as Carstairs, doesn't it? If Carstairs never patronised the hotel under that name, the manager wouldn't recognise him as Knight. I looked out of Mrs White's window, at her suggestion, when I visited her and I wouldn't guarantee to recognise anybody who got down from the coach, so *she* need not have made the connection.'

'We had better find out whether Carstairs ever visited the hotel. If he did, he certainly cannot be Knight.'

'We're suspicious of Knight, it seems. Why should we be?'

'A precautionary attitude only. He may be as innocent (and as dead) as Noone and Daigh. On the other hand, he may be their murderer. His "illness" is a suspicious circumstance in itself. If he is a guilty man he might find it convenient to "disappear" in order to lead us to assume that he, too, had been murdered.'

'Why would he want us to assume that?'

'If he is the murderer or an accomplice it might be to his advantage that the police should waste valuable time in looking for him in the wrong place. Noone was murdered near Hulliwell Hall and his body found there. This finding of the body was not part of the murderers' plan and must have given them food for thought. Then it must be known by now that Daigh's body also has been found, again in the place where he was last known to be alive. The criminals had to make a hasty revision of their plans, I think, for they had counted upon a long period of search and doubt, with perhaps no police activity at all if it were taken for granted that the drivers had disappeared voluntarily.'

'So the situation, as they saw it once the bodies were found, demanded a third disappearance which might indicate a third murder, you think, and while the police who, because of the discovery of the bodies, are now hot-foot on the trail, go chasing around Saighdearan and Fort William, the murderers are sitting pretty in some quite other place. Where, do you suppose?'

'I think we must leave that to the police to find out. There is little we can do about the matter now, except to suggest that they get on the track of Carstairs, of whom, no doubt, McFee and the Whites, between them, can furnish a reasonably accurate description. If this description of Carstairs appears to tally with Basil Honfleur's and the women clerks' description of Knight, our part in this matter would appear to be over, but I am sure they are not the same man.'

'You *do* think Vittorio was young Wullie's black man, don't you?'

'I will not commit myself as to that, but it is possible, as perhaps I have already indicated.'

Back at the hotel Dame Beatrice asked for an interview with the manager.

'Did Mr Carstairs, from one of those bungalows on the hillside above the hotel, ever come in here for a meal or to drink at the bar?' she asked.

'Carstairs? I wouldn't know him,' the manager replied.

'Did Driver Knight always bring the County Motors coach here?'

'Only once before, I believe. Two men called Ford and Dibbens alternated with the tour.'

'Will you describe Knight as closely as ever you can? It may be vitally important.'

CHAPTER 10

The Bungalow

'Describe him?' The manager looked dubious. 'My dining-room staff would be better at that than I would. We get coaches all the time during the summer and unless the drivers have any complaints, which is very seldom indeed at my hotel, I don't really see anything of them. They're civil, unobtrusive lads as a rule and they don't bring themselves much to my notice. Why not have a wee word with my head waiter?'

The head waiter was Swiss. Like most of his calling, he had a good command of English and he readily consented to describe Knight.

'This driver was taller than myself. I am metres one point seven. I think maybe he would be seven centimetres taller.'

'Two and a half to three inches taller than yourself, and you measure roughly five feet seven. I see. What kind of build has he?'

'Build? His body? Not fat.'

'Noticeably broad-shouldered, powerful?'

'Oh, no, not that; just ordinary. He had brown hair, a little grey on the temples and cut short, not the modern fashion.'

'Was he clean-shaven?'

'Oh, yes, there was no moustache or beard.'

'What kind of man was he?'

'Jocund, always with a smile.'

112

'Did you like him?'

The Swiss shrugged his shoulders.

'What does your Shakespeare say?' he asked rhetorically. Dame Beatrice cackled.

'*Was* he a smiling villain?' she said, 'or are you referring to Julius Caesar's preference for fat men?'

The head waiter merely shrugged his expressive shoulders again.

'He had been here only once before,' he said, as though this unhelpful remark was an answer to her question.

'He was in your dining room on the first night the party stayed here?'

'Making himself very agreeable to the ladies, yes.'

'And you saw him at dinner the evening the party returned from Skye?'

'Certainly I did. The people at his table invited him to a glass of wine and I myself took their order, so I know he was there.'

'He did not take coffee in the lounge that evening, I am told.'

'I do not know about that. He had to look over the coach, perhaps.'

'Would anybody on the staff know whether he took the coach out after dinner, I wonder?'

The head waiter did not know, but he thought not. However, he went off to make enquiries and returned shortly to say that nobody believed that the coach had been moved that night.

'Nothing to show that it couldn't have been moved after dark, though, and brought back before morning,' said Laura, when she and Dame Beatrice were alone. 'I mean, *something* happened that night, otherwise Knight would not have disappeared. I'm beginning to wonder more and more whether he *is* the nigger in our woodpile. You don't think, failing any gatehouses in the immediate neighbourhood, that the murderers did a Young Hunting on him, do you?'

'Your cryptic reference eludes me.'

'The Border ballad, you know:

The deepest pot in Clyde Water
They got Young Hunting in,
With a green turf tied across his breast
To keep that good lord down.

'That's all I meant. I don't suppose it would be past
somebody's ingenuity to stab the man the way Noone and
Daigh were stabbed, take him by night to White's boatyard,
commandeer a boat and take the body down the loch towards
Oban and drop it overboard. If it was weighted down, it could lie
on the bed of the loch till Doomsday and nobody except the
murderer would know it was there.'

'You may be right.'

'Things do go in threes, you know.'

'I still think we were brought up here to get us away from
those areas in Derbyshire and Pembrokeshire where our enquiries were beginning to prove embarrassing to somebody.'

'But if you thought that, why did you come?'

'To allay suspicion.'

'Whose?'

'Ah, yes, whose?'

'Well, what's the next move?'

'I think I should like to find out for certain whether the head
waiter's Mr Knight is Mrs White's Mr Carstairs.'

'I thought you'd made up your mind that they are two
different men.'

'I should wish to be sure. We now have an unbiased description of Knight from the headwaiter. He does not know
Carstairs. Mrs White, we assume, does not know Knight, so a
comparison of height and the general appearance of the two men
may be of interest.'

'And if the descriptions don't tally, as you believe they
won't?'

'Then I may be impelled to accept your Young Hunting
theory.'

'You'll never find the body if they *have* dumped it in Loch Linnhe. Once past Sallachan Point, goodness knows how deep it is out in the middle. It's ten fathoms through the Narrows and then the marine contour lines pretty well follow the line of the shore. If they did weight the body . . .'

'We are assuming that there *is* a body, you know. Do you care to accompany me to Mrs White's again?'

They mounted the slope. This time a youthful maidservant answered the door. Dame Beatrice produced a card.

'Please to come ben,' said the girl. She admitted them and left them in the narrow entrance hall while she went to show the card to her mistress. Mrs White received them effusively.

'I did not know I would have the pleasure again, Dame Beatrice,' she said. 'My husband is at work, of course. He will be sorry to have missed you. Is there any more news?'

'There seems to be a discrepancy,' Dame Beatrice replied. 'We have received two descriptions of the man for whom we are enquiring. Of course, neither may be correct, but it would help our enquiry if you will give us your own description of Mr Carstairs.'

'I had very little to do with him, you know. He was here to-day, gone tomorrow – that kind of thing. That is why we thought he might be a commercial traveller, or perhaps be going around to sell his pictures.'

'Was he tall, short, fat, thin, dark, fair?'

'Oh, you just want *that* kind of description. I should call him about medium, taking him all round, I suppose. He was on the sturdy side and had brown hair. I don't know what colour his eyes were, but I expect they were either brown or grey. He was taller than me, but not as tall as my husband. Mr White is five feet ten.'

'Did you ever see your husband and Mr Carstairs standing together?'

'No, I don't think so, but I'm sure Mr Carstairs wasn't as tall.'

'And he was a sturdy type of man? — broad-shouldered, noticeably strongly built?'

'No, just ordinary I think. Oh, I don't know, though. Come to think, he had very broad shoulders and I believe he must have been very strong because once' — she giggled in a girlishly repellent fashion — 'I had a garment blow off my line of washing and go sailing over the back fence, so, instead of going all the way round, I decided to climb the fence to get it back and my foot got stuck between the railings. Well, I knew Mr Carstairs was at home, so I yelled and shouted and he came out and reached up and lifted me straight into the air to release my shoe — and I weigh all of eleven and a half stone, you know.'

'Presumably you have heard him speak, then?'

'Oh, yes. He had to, on that occasion, didn't he? He had quite a gentlemanly kind of voice, quite public school, you know. If he *was* a commercial traveller he was a very high class sort of one, I should say. But, of course, he was an artist as well.'

'But you never saw any of his paintings? He never attempted to interest you in his work?'

'Oh, no. He was not the type of man to take advantage' — she giggled again — 'not of *any* sort.'

'How unenterprising of him! Tell me, Mrs White — you must know your husband's boat-yard pretty well — would it be possible for anybody to get into it after dark and borrow a boat?'

'Oh, I daresay you could get into the yard easy enough, but it wouldn't do you much good. My husband hasn't got any big boats with properly bedded engines. His are all little things with outboard motors and those are all removed and locked up at night. Then he's got one or two small yachts, but the sails are all stowed in the sail lockers while they're at the boat-yard.'

'But if you owned a car and your own outboard motor, you could make shift to borrow a boat and then put it back without anybody being the wiser?'

'No, I don't believe you could,' said Mrs White. 'There are guard dogs at the next yard and I'm sure they'd create if anybody got into my husband's place after dark.'

'Guard dogs? I thought everybody trusted everybody else in the Highlands.'

'There was a gang of roughs – Glasgow Irish – up here on the spree the year before last and a lot of damage was done, that's why the dogs are there.'

'I see. When was Mr Carstairs last in residence next door?'

'He drove off in his car the day before the party went to Skye. He drove off at about mid-day and they pulled in for the night at about six and went to Skye the next morning, like I told you before.'

'And the driver disappeared some time that same night. I see.'

'So Willie wasn't drowned in Yarrow,' said Laura,' if the murderer didn't commandeer a boat, and so the chances are that he is still alive.'

'We cannot assume that. I had hoped to be able to prove that Knight spent the time when he was supposed to be on sick leave in carrying out those smuggling operations which, rightly or wrongly, I have assumed to be at the bottom of this business. It seems now that we must adjust our ideas.'

'Yes, I see that; but if Carstairs isn't Knight, who is he? If he isn't Knight – and we can take that for granted after the descriptions we've had of both of them – he may not be mixed up in this business at all. You said, a while ago, that you thought we'd been persuaded to come up here on a wild-goose chase. Isn't it time we went back and had another word with Basil Honfleur about Knight?'

'You may well be right. Let us sleep on it. I will make up my mind in the morning.'

Laura guessed that Dame Beatrice was dissatisfied with their progress. The theory that Knight and Carstairs were the same person had appeared promising, although, except for Knight's sick leave and Carstairs' comings and goings, there had been little to support it. Now, however, there seemed no way to connect the two men. Knight might or might not still be alive; Carstairs might or might not be the commercial traveller and/or the roving artist that Mrs White took him to be. The only suspicious circumstance about him, in fact, was that, as he seemed to be in residence there so seldom and so intermittently, he should have purchased a bungalow in Saighdearan at all, considering that there were a hotel and a motel on the spot which he could use.

In any case, thought Laura, lying fully dressed, except for her shoes, on her comfortable hotel bed at eleven o'clock that night, Saighdearan seemed an unlikely place for a commercial traveller to buy a *pied-à-terre,* although it might suit an artist.

'I'm still sure we're right, and there's more to our Mr Carstairs than meets the eye,' said Laura, to the four walls of her room, 'and I'm dashed if I don't go and have a snoop around that place of his.'

When, having put on her shoes and an anorak when she had changed her dinner-frock for slacks and a sweater, she got into the hotel yard, the last of the bar customers were leaving and there was conversation, laughter and much revving up of cars.

Laura strolled out on to the road, crossed to the loch-side footpath and strolled onwards in the direction of Fort William.

The night was luminous, although there was only the sliver of a new moon. The waters of the loch washed very gently towards the stony shores, stirred slightly by a night-wind and the far-off tides beyond Lismore Island and Oban.

Gradually the noise of the cars died away as the customers of the hotel bar made their homeward journeys. Laura strolled on, enjoying the night air and the blessed silence of stars, mountains and the deep, dark water, the latter flashing now and again into moon-tipped wavelets as the currents made their infinitesimal movements.

Except for an occasional car which swept by at speed along the otherwise deserted road, she might have been alone in the world. On the other side of the loch was the awful majesty of the Ardgour mountains. In front of her lay Lochaber and somewhere away to the east was the vast Killiechonate Forest and the awe-inspiring massif of Ben Nevis.

It occurred to Laura that it might be interesting to pay a visit to MacGregor White's boatyard, but then she remembered the guard dogs near by who could be trusted to give warning of her approach. Besides, except that they were Carstairs' only near neighbours, there was nothing to connect the Whites with him, so she began to retrace her steps towards the hotel and, when she reached the spot opposite the lane which led up to the two bungalows, she crossed the road and began the steep ascent.

There were no lights in the Whites' bungalow. Laura opened the gate which led to Carstairs' front door and took to the small lawn to avoid the sound of her footsteps on the path. The path continued, however, round the side of the building away from the Whites' property, so she followed it round to the back.

Whether the bungalow was empty, or whether the occupant was in residence again, there was no way of telling except by knocking on the door and this Laura, who could think of no reason she could give for calling at such an hour, was unwilling to risk. Having conceived the idea of inspecting the interior, however, she was hoping to find some means of ingress, regardless of the chance of being caught in the criminal act of breaking and entering, or whatever that was called under Scottish law. Herself a Highlander by birth and ancestry, she still had little knowledge of the legal terminology of her native land.

Cautiously she tried the back door, but it was locked. This appeared to indicate that the bungalow was empty of human kind, for few people in the Highlands, as in the English countryside, trouble to lock up, even at night, if the house is tenanted.

There were three windows at the back of the bungalow. Laura, prowling past them, diagnosed them as belonging to kitchen, bedroom and bathroom. A side window which she passed could be that of a second bedroom, she thought. She ignored it, since from it the light from a small torch she had brought with her could be seen from the road if anybody was passing. At the back of the bungalow, however, apart from a very small garden, there was nothing but the hillside, so, having halted and listened for a while, she switched on the torch and inspected the back windows.

Her conclusions, so far as the kitchen and the bedroom were concerned, proved to be correct and, as the third window was made of opaque glass, she decided that she was right about that also. It was the only sash window, she noticed; the other two were casements. It was almost as though it had been put in especially for her purpose.

'Oh, well, here goes for the bathroom, then,' thought Laura. 'Better take my shoes off.' She did this, laid them on the sill of the adjacent bedroom window and, taking a stout bowie knife from the pocket of her anorak, she slipped back the catch of the bathroom window. 'Here, I expect, is where I break my neck,' she thought, as she pushed up the lower sash.

Kneeling on the narrow sill, she shone her torch into the room. Fortunately the window was fairly wide and it was not above either the bath or the washbasin. The lid of the WC, which was directly under the window, was down. This was an unexpected bit of luck. Her stockinged foot slipped on the wooden lid of the WC but she held on, retained her balance and stepped down on to the bathroom floor.

The bathroom door was locked on the inside. This seemed a curious circumstance. It looked as though the last occupant of the bungalow must have left it by the same means as Laura had managed to enter it. She turned the key, waited and listened and then opened the door.

Feeling that in for a penny was in for a pound, she tried the door which was next to the bathroom. It opened into a bedroom and here all was confusion. The bedclothes and two pillows were on the floor, the mattress was half on and half off the bed, a small cupboard on the wall was wide open and so were the drawers of a dressing chest.

Laura shone her torch round and about, took in the scene and then continued her exploration of the bungalow. But for the sitting-room, which appeared to have no key, all the rooms (the bathroom having been the sole exception) were locked on the outside, so at every door she listened carefully before she turned the key and went in, but nowhere else was in the same state of disorder as the bedroom she had entered.

'Wonder whether they found what they were looking for?' she said aloud. She returned to the bedroom. As it overlooked the hillside and not the road, she judged that it would be safe to switch on the electric light. She did this and then noticed what the beam of her torch had been too limited in scope to disclose. The tumbled bedclothes were stained with blood.

'Here's a nice how d'ye do!' muttered Laura. The thought that she was unlawfully on enclosed premises with every chance of being in company with a dead body was not an encouraging one. Still less encouraging, because it changed speculation into certainty, was the sight of a black shoe and a sock-clad ankle sticking out from under the tumbled bed.

CHAPTER 11

Pistol and Dagger

There was a telephone in the hall. Laura's first instinct was to ring up the police, but she realised that Dame Beatrice, whose hearing remained unimpaired by age, would have heard her leave her room. She would probably sit up and read until one o'clock in the morning and, long before that, would anticipate Laura's return, so she looked up the number of the hotel and rang the office.

'I want to speak to Dame Beatrice Lestrange Bradley,' she said.

'Who is that speaking?'

'Her secretary, Mrs Gavin.'

'I will put you through.'

'I say, Dame B,' said Laura, when they were connected and she heard her employer's voice come over the line, I'm stuck here at Carstairs' bungalow until the police come, so don't worry if I'm kept here half the night. I've found a body.'

'Whose?'

'I don't know. I only saw a man's shoe and a bit of his sock, but there's blood all over the place.'

'I see. You have kept all the rules except that against breaking and entering, I hope.'

'I haven't touched a thing except a window sash, door-keys

and one electric light switch, if that's what you mean. I'm now going to ring the police.'

'Do nothing so foolish. Wipe your fingerprints off that telephone and come back here at once.'

'And my other prints?'

'Wipe them off if you know what you have touched, but hurry here. I will explain when I see you.'

'Right.' Laura did as she was told, left the bungalow by the bathroom window, which she had left open, and returned to the hotel.

'Why hadn't I to ring up the police?' she asked.

'Because I have just done so myself. There is no point in your having to confess to an illegal act, still less that you have been on premises which house a dead body. Your telephone call to me must be regarded as an anonymous one. You may leave the necessary evasions to me. Meanwhile, change those clothes for the dress you wore at dinner. When the police arrive . . .'

'Won't they go straight to Carstairs' bungalow?'

'I think not. I have told them that the dead man may be the coach-driver we are looking for and, if so, that the manager here will be able to identify him and that, with the information I have gained, I should be able, with your help, to confirm that identification.'

'Why should anybody ring you up and not ourselves?' asked the inspector, when he arrived in company with a sergeant.

'I should imagine that whoever it was left me to communicate with you rather than involve himself directly. Besides, by this time, everybody in the neighbourhood probably knows my errand, which is to find this missing coach-driver.'

'And ye'll be thinking that somebody else has found him?'

'It is not impossible. He disappeared from this hotel.'

'Aye.' The hotel manager, who was drinking a quiet nightcap in his private sitting-room, was told to stand by in case he was wanted and, accompanied by Laura, Dame Beatrice went with the police to the bungalow. The inspector cut a small pane of glass out of the front door, reached for the knob inside which operated the lock and in they all went.

'Did your caller say in which room the body was to be found?' the inspector enquired when he had closed the front door and switched on the hall light.

'No,' Dame Beatrice truthfully replied, for this information had not been supplied by Laura over the telephone. ('I admired that answer of yours. It was given, like Kipling says, "with steadfastness and *careful* truth," ' Laura commented later).

'Oh, well, the bungalow isna a' that lairge. We'll find it soon enough if it's here,' the inspector remarked. 'Will ye kindly bide here while I look around?'

He was back with them in a few minutes.

'It is true, then?' Dame Beatrice enquired.

'Och, aye, it is true enough, although I'm not surprised ye were sceptical. Whoever did it had pushed the body under the bed. It's naebody we ken, so maybe you would tak' a look at it yourself, ma'am and tell us do you recognise it. It's no sie a terrible sight. A quick stab in the back by somebody wha kenned juist whaur to plant a knife. The doctor will be here directly, but there's nae doubt about what happened.'

'No signs of a struggle?'

'The mon was taken unaware, maist likely, but the intruder was a burglar. The room's in an awfu' mess.'

'Have you found the weapon?'

'We have not. We dinna look for that kind of help frae murderers.'

Dame Beatrice and Laura followed him into the bedroom. The bed had been pulled away from the wall by the police, leaving the corpse where it had been so rudely thrust. It was clad in pyjama trousers, shoes and socks, and was lying on its face so that the angry gash in its back was clearly visible in the strong electric light.

'Do ye put a name on him?' asked the inspector. Dame Beatrice and Laura exchanged glances, but said nothing. 'There is no reason not to move him,' the inspector continued, 'since he has been moved already. Turn him over, sergeant.' The sergeant obliged, and both Dame Beatrice and Laura recognised the man immediately. The inspector went on: 'We'll need to get MacDonald frae the hotel to take a look at him, I daresay, and I maun rouse the couple next door. They should be able to help us, I think, to put a name on him.'

'By the way, Inspector,' said Dame Beatrice, 'I suppose the bloodstains on the bedding will be analysed?'

'Analysed? For what purpose, ma'am? There's nae doubt they came from the wound in the deid mon's back.'

'There is probably no doubt at all, but it might be interesting to make sure.'

The inspector looked perplexed.

'I ken well that ye've a great reputation, ma'am,' he said, 'so a hint from you is as good as a nod, as they say. Will ye no tell me what is in your mind?'

'Nothing, except that I believe in making certain that what we take as evidence really *is* evidence, that is all. I mean, suppose this blood proves to correspond with that of the dead man, well and good. But suppose, for the sake of argument, that his blood happened to belong to a different group, would that not cause us to think that this death is not the result of murder but of a fight to the death in which the assailant was also wounded?'

The inspector scratched his head, but promised that the comparison should be carried out.

'And now what about the identification?' he asked.

'He is not the missing coach-driver,' said Dame Beatrice, "but I have seen this man before. I do not know his full name. He was introduced to me merely as Vittorio. He is a one-time friend of Mr Honfleur of County Coaches. Incidentally, the nature of the wound, its position and the fact that only one blow appears to have been struck, relate it to the other two bodies I have seen.'

'Aye. Well, if it is the mon ye say, maybe MacDonald at the hotel will not know him. Weel, now, ye'd like to get to your beds, yoursel' and Mistress Gavin, but before ye leave, tell me what you make of these.'

He whipped up the pyjama jacket which matched the trousers the corpse was wearing. It was lying on the bedside table as though the man had discarded it during the night, but when the inspector twitched it aside there seemed little doubt that it had been placed on the bedside table to hide what lay beneath.

'I dinna ken what the thief was looking for, the way he had the place turned upside down,' the inspector said, 'but if it was these wee pistols, well, he didna look in the right place. We found them on the floor between the body and the wall.'

Dame Beatrice did not need a warning not to touch the exhibits. She produced a magnifying glass and studied them closely.

'I am not an expert in these matters,' she said, 'but these very fine pistols were made, I should say, during the late seventeenth century. They remind me very much of a pair I have seen in the White Tower of London. If I am not mistaken, they are the work of Pierre Monlong, a Huguenot gunmaker who was appointed Gentleman Armourer to Dutch William, the husband of that Princess Mary who was the daughter of King James the Second and who became joint sovereign of England in 1689 with her husband.'

'Ye call him Dutch William,' said the inspector. Dame Beatrice waved a yellow claw.

'A resolute man,' she said. 'Queen Elizabeth Tudor would not have liked him. There is no doubt that he usurped his wife's rights. Be that as it may, the gunmaker Pierre Monlong previously had held the post, as such, to the royal house of France and was a master of his craft. Note the delicate scroll-work on these pistols and the inlays in gold on pale blue enamel. These are not so much weapons of offence as works of art, Inspector.'

'They would be collectors' items, then.'

'Very valuable ones. The pair I saw at the Tower were valued at ninety thousand pounds.'

'Losh! Ye dinna tell me that!'

'It is true. However, I doubt whether our burglar knew of the existence of these treasures. The devastation he has left behind him seems to indicate that he was certainly looking for something, but – tell me, Inspector, have you had any burglaries of *objets d'art* in this neighbourhood recently?'

'Aye, and no lang syne. Some Americans have Castle Bratach this summer and they reported thefts of valuable china, but, so far as I know, nobody has reported losing a pair of pistols.'

'I may be able to trace them in England. Well, if you don't need us any longer we will accept your permission to leave. I should be pleased to know the full identity of this dead man Vittorio.'

'If MacDonald or White can identify him, you shall be told, ma'am. Otherwise we may need to call upon Mr Honfleur.'

The manager of the hotel could not identify the dead man.

'And the Whites?' asked Dame Beatrice of the manager, for whose return to the hotel she had waited up.

'They could not put a name on him,' said MacDonald, 'any more than I can. All they could tell the police is that he is not the man they know as Carstairs.'

'He wore surprisingly large pyjamas,' said Dame Beatrice, 'and apparently went to bed in his shoes.'

On the following morning Laura drove Dame Beatrice southward to Oban and across the Border to Carlisle, where they were to spend the night. The next day they went south again as far as Cheltenham and on the afternoon following a night there they reached Dame Beatrice's New Forest home.

'Well, I suppose it's all over, so far as we are concerned,' said Laura, after they had enjoyed one of Henri's superb dinners. She twirled the brandy in her glass and looked across at her employer. 'Aren't you feeling rather sorry?' she asked.

'No,' Dame Beatrice replied. 'For one thing, it is not all over so far as we are concerned. We have not found Knight, which is what we went to Saighdearan to do. However, I am glad to be back in England and shall enjoy a chat with Basil Honfleur. Then I shall resume the search for Knight. As for Basil himself, the evening is still young, so perhaps you will engage him on the telephone and suggest that he come to see us as soon as he can. We ourselves have done enough travelling for the time being and we know that he is not particularly busy at this time in the season.'

'He'll be out to dinner most likely, but I'll try.'

'Leave it until ten. He should be at home by then.'

This was so. Laura made contact and Honfleur was bidden to come to lunch at the Stone House on the following day.

'What is the news?' he asked, as soon as he arrived.

'We came back from Scotland yesterday and have left the whole matter in the hands of the police,' replied Dame Beatrice.

'You mean you are backing out?'

'Yes, if you care to put it like that. There is nothing more for us to do until a man who calls himself Carstairs is found. But let us relax over lunch and then we shall tell you all.'

'You had some success, then, at Fort William?'

'I would not put it so positively.'

When lunch was over and coffee had been served, Honfleur refused to contain himself any longer.

'Come on, now, Dame Beatrice, *please*!' he said. 'What happened up there, and what did you find out?'

'But little,' Dame Beatrice replied. This was greatly to Laura's surprise, for she had expected that Honfleur would at least be told that Vittorio had been found murdered. She knew better, however, than to mention this herself, and Dame Beatrice proceeded to give Honfleur a detailed description of the rest of their activities on the shores of Loch Linnhe. Laura added her quota whenever her employer turned the narrative over to her and, as the recital proceeded, Honfleur looked more and more sceptical, but he waited until it was finished before he put in a word.

'I still can't follow why you identified Carstairs with Knight,' he said.

'What makes you think that I did?' Dame Beatrice enquired. 'The descriptions of the two men do not tally. All the same, there are factors which make me highly suspicious of Knight. The *times* fit all too well.'

'How do you mean? What times?' asked Honfleur.

'Knight has been on sick leave.'

'We had a medical certificate, you know.'

'One only?'

'Well, yes, but we allow the chaps a lot of leeway. They get stomach ulcers, you see, so, if we get a medical certificate to say so, we trust the driver to come back when he feels fit enough, and of course we pay him while he's away from work. Luckily, although I told you we are a subsidiary of the bus company, we're independent of them so far as our treatment of our workers is concerned and so we can make our own rules.'

'I see. Well, how long was Knight away before he took the coach up to Scotland?'

'Three weeks altogether.'

'During those three weeks a coach was "borrowed" and two of your drivers were killed.'

'A nasty coincidence, but a coincidence nevertheless. I'm certain of it.'

'Your drivers are long-service, responsible men, yet one of them moves, or allows to be moved, his coach from the entrance to Hulliwell Hall, and the same kind of thing happens at Dantwylch. In each case the driver is murdered. Do you think Noone and Daigh would have allowed any casual stranger to move (or to persuade them to move) the coach for which they were responsible?'

'No, of course not.'

'But if a mate of theirs – you told me that your drivers are a close-knit little community — if one of their own comrades begged them, as a favour, to move the coach, might they not, knowing that their passengers were safely occupied for anything from an hour to an hour and a half, have complied with what I have no doubt seemed to be a reasonable request?'

'Well, I suppose, if you put it like that . . .'

'I do put it like that.'

'Oh, dear! But I still don't believe Knight was involved in all this.'

'Who else, then?'

'Well, a driver from another company, I suppose. It's known that there were other coaches, besides ours, at Hulliwell Hall and at Dantwylch on the days in question.'

'Have it your own way for the present. Knight then returns to work . . .'

'To help us out, remember.'

'Possibly. I understand, though, that he did not usually take the tour up to Fort William.'

'Well, no, but I can assure you he did not suggest the trip to me. I asked him whether he would be willing to deputise for Ford, whom I wanted for the Brittany tour, as he's done it before —'

'What about Driver Dibbens? Is he not Ford's partner? I understood that they alternated.'

'I was very glad to rest Dibbens. He's had more than his share of extra work since we lost Noone and Daigh and while Knight himself was on sick leave.'

'Were your drivers, any of them, acquainted with your erstwhile friend Vittorio?'

Honfleur stared at her.

'Please don't call him my friend,' he said. 'I never really took to the fellow. He was useful, merely. Had a nose for antiques, and could manage to pick up things I wanted much cheaper than I could have got them for myself, even if I'd known where to look for them. It was because of what Miss Mendel reported to you that I severed my connection with him. I only hope she was telling the truth about what she was shown at his digs. Do you think she was?'

'Yes. You have not answered my question.'

'Well, yes, some of my drivers did know him. I used to reserve him a seat on a coach whenever he asked me to do so. He would go on a coach which was only half to three quarters booked up so that there was room in the boot to bring back anything he was able to find for me.'

'And for himself, no doubt. How often did he travel with Knight?'

'Not more than with several of the others.'

'But he *did* travel with him. Where?'

'Oh, when Knight was on the East Anglia tour he went with him, and on some of the West Country tours.'

'But not to Scotland?'

'No. Knight never did the Scottish tours except the one to Edinburgh and the Trossachs.'

'I understood that he had been once before to Saighdearan, and that cannot have been more than a year or two ago, since the hotel is almost new.'

'Perhaps you're right, but, you know, Dame Beatrice, I do honestly think you're making bricks without straw.'

'The Israelites, faced with a similar situation, had to gather their own straw. Allow me to do likewise.'

'You suspect Knight of murdering two of his fellow drivers? But I'm sure that's quite ridiculous.'

'I don't think Honfleur was exactly enamoured of your conclusions,' said Laura, when he had left them. 'Why didn't you tell him that Vittorio has been murdered, too?'

'He will know soon enough. I do not wish to spread that particular bit of news until it is released to the newspapers.'

'And what else?'

Dame Beatrice cackled and did not reply, so Laura continued:

'It seems to me that you've got something up your sleeve, as usual. What do you know that I don't – apart from the value of those pistols? Funny the killer didn't find them, seeing how he had ransacked that bungalow.'

'He did not find them because he was not looking for them. I do not think he had any idea that they were there.'

'What *was* he looking for, then?'

'Probably some incriminating documents.'

With this unsatisfactory answer Laura found she had to be content, so all she said was:

'Oh, well, all we can do is to wait upon events, I suppose.'

Events were not long in coming. Laura, who never needed more than three to four hours of sleep a night, was wide awake when the sounds downstairs caused her to sit up in bed and listen. Then she crept out on to the landing and listened again. She returned to her room, pulled slacks and a sweater over her pyjamas and laced up a pair of stout but rubber-soled shoes before she made her way to her employer's bedroom. Dame Beatrice, partly because of her medical training and partly because it came naturally at her advanced age, was a light sleeper. She sat up the moment Laura turned the handle of the door.

'Don't show a light,' murmured Laura. 'Visitors downstairs.'

'I expected them,' Dame Beatrice murmured in response. 'Leave my door ajar.' She fished a small revolver out from under her pillow, slid out of bed and pulled on her dressing-gown and slippers. 'Into the cupboard with you.'

The Stone House had been built in an age when the principal bedrooms needed an annexe in the form of a powder closet. That which was attached to Dame Beatrice's room was large and airy and had a small window which overlooked the drive. Laura went over to this as Dame Beatrice quickly rearranged the bed, then extracted the key from the lock of the powder-room drawer and brought it in with her, but did not quite close the door. 'Not burglars?' Laura asked, *sotto voce* again.

'I think not. Listen!' The Stone House possessed a creaking stair. Dame Beatrice, whose life had been threatened more than once by the friends and relatives of persons she had helped to get (in the old days) hanged or (nowadays) put away, had realised the value of this stair and had allowed it to remain as a useful kind of watchdog. Sure enough the intruder trod on it as he made his stealthy progress upwards and it gave its usual warning. There was a slight exclamation, quickly stifled, and then the bedroom door creaked in its turn.

Laura tensed herself. Dame Beatrice cocked her revolver. A faint, grey, late summer dawn was already beginning to break and she always opened her curtains when she was ready to get into bed, so that, although it was still too dark to recognise the intruder, it was just possible to follow his shadowy movements as he crossed over to the bed.

A couple of grunts and a couple of heavy blows indicated his purpose. Dame Beatrice gave an eldritch screech, shouted, 'Hands up!' and fired a couple of blanks into the room. There was a hoarse yell, the intruder leapt to the bedroom window, forced up the lower sash and dropped out into the garden.

'Stay where you are,' said Dame Beatrice to Laura. 'He may not be alone.' But the next moment there was the sound of a car being started up.

'Didn't break his neck, anyway,' said Laura. There was a pounding of feet on the staircase and a voice shouted with Gallic urgency,

'Madame! Madame! Montrez-moi le gredin! Où est le scélérat?'

'Gone like the dew from off the grass,' Dame Beatrice replied, switching on the bedroom light. She stooped and picked up something from the floor. Laura uttered a gargling cry and, ignoring the object which Dame Beatrice had retrieved from where the intruder, in his efforts to force open the window, had dropped it on the carpet, pointed dramatically at the bed.

'What – what – what on earth!' she said.

'That?' said her employer, leering indulgently at the object under the counterpane. 'Oh, that is my *doppelgänger.*'

'Good heavens! You mustn't say that sort of thing, even in jest!' said Laura, horrified. She subjected the counterfeit Dame Beatrice to scrutiny. She saw the vague outline of a thin body under the coverlet. On the pillow was a wig of black hair. A *papier mâché* head to which it was attached had been smashed to pieces.

'Good God!' exclaimed Laura, horrified.

'The Sherlock Holmes touch,' said Dame Beatrice complacently. 'I had time to slip it into the bed before I joined you in the cupboard. But observe! We have a prize.' She displayed the object she had retrieved from the carpet. It was a Commando fighting knife, a thin-bladed, double-edged, workmanlike little weapon with a black, cast-metal hilt topped by a brass knob. The grip was slightly indented with a series of criss-cross patterns to render it non-slip and at the top of the blade, which was about seven inches long and tapered to a sharp point, there was engraved on one side the makers' name, that of a pre-eminent maker of razor-blades, and on the other the initials F – S and the words Fighting Knife.

'He came well-prepared,' said Laura grimly. 'First a coshing and then a stabbing. You know, the odd thing is that there was something about him – of course one only got an impression – do *you* know who he was?'

'I believe so.'

'You'll have to charge him.'

'On the strength of a doubtful recognition in the grey light which precedes the dawn?'

'Fingerprints on the knife, then.'

'I have overlaid them with my own.'

'That wouldn't fox the police.'

'No, perhaps not, but I am sure he would have taken the precaution of wearing gloves. Besides, I want him arrested for actual murder, not for a clumsy attempt at it. I think that, if this little episode means anything, it means that the murderer of Noone and Daigh . . .'

'And possibly Knight . . .'

'Is becoming alarmed, and that indicates that, whether we are aware of it or not, we are making progress.'

'What I should like to know is how he got wise to you. I mean, I know that your name has been mentioned in connection with the inquest on Noone, but why should this thug believe you to be so dangerous to him that he sets out to kill you? He doesn't even know I broke into that bungalow.'

'All the same, he must know that we went to Saighdearan and have been told of a mysterious foreigner who spoke to the boy at the hotel.'

'You *will* report to the police, though, won't you? He may not stop at one attempt and the rôle of guard-dog to a hunted fawn has never appealed to me. I would much rather the police took over.'

'Oh, yes, I shall report to the police, but I shall not inform them that I believe I recognised the man. For one thing, that would not suit my plans and, for another, they might not believe me. We must not be too precipitate at this juncture. I shall simply tell them that a man broke in and made his escape in a car.'

'After trying to murder you.'

'Since I was never in danger, that fact need not emerge.'

'But suppose he tries again?'

'Like Antonio, I am armed and well prepared.'

'Are you going to tell me who you think it was?'

'Your guess is as good as mine, and, in that semi-darkness, both of us may have guessed wrongly.'

'Neither of us has ever seen Knight,' said Laura thoughtfully.

CHAPTER 12

No Coaches on the Roads

There was a long pause. Dame Beatrice looked enquiringly at her secretary, but realised that the pause was a pause for thought. At last Laura raised her eyes and spread out her hands in a gesture of helplessness.

'Ah!' said Dame Beatrice, with satisfaction. 'I wondered when you were going to ask me that.'

Laura, accustomed as she was to having her mind read, gaped at her employer and then grinned.

'Oh, no,' she said. 'You don't catch me out like that. Just *what* do you think I'm going to ask you?'

'If this Commando dagger, with its blade which must measure, midway down the length, at least seven-tenths of an inch across, was used to assassinate Noone and Daigh.'

'So what's the answer?'

'I do not know, and I am not prepared to guess.' Her tone was so final that Laura said,

'I don't think I'll bother to go back to bed. How early can we telephone the police about this break-in?'

'There is no hurry. Contact them after breakfast, if you will.'

'There's another point which is bothering me a bit, you know.'

'Oh, dear! You mean our intruder's acumen.'

'Yes, that's it. From the moment I heard the first sounds downstairs, right up to the moment I came in here, into your room, not more than a minute or two could have passed.'

'Indeed? Yes, I expect you are right.'

'Well, now, how did this man, with five bedrooms and your upstairs consulting-room to choose from, come straightway to where you were sleeping?'

'That is, presuming I was the person he intended to murder. What did you think of the wig I had spread so artistically over the pillow? One learns a great deal from the Sherlock Holmes stories, does one not? The dog which did nothing in the night? The life-like bust which appeared to throw a perfect silhouette of Holmes' profile against the window-blind?'

'When are you going to see Honfleur again?' asked Laura, dismissing these questions as persiflage.

'When our night visitor has had time to realise that I am not proposing to give his name to the police. I might, however, ask *you* to go and see Mr Honfleur.'

'But you *are* going to report the break-in?'

'It is my duty as a citizen to do so,' replied Dame Beatrice solemnly. 'Well, off to your bath, or whatever you intend to do before breakfast. I am for bed.' She removed the black wig which was attached to the smashed mask, excavated a kind of Guy Fawkes figure encased in hessian from beneath the coverlet, placed the lot in a vast oak chest at the foot of the bed, retired to rest and resumed her light slumbers. Laura went down the garden to the well-screened swimming pool, discarded her pyjamas and dived in.

' "I am sent," ' quoted Laura to a worried Basil Honfleur, ' "with broom before, to sweep the dust behind the door." Or, of course, under the carpet, just as Dame B's policy may dictate.'

'Her policy? She told me on the telephone that an attempt had been made on her life. Can that possibly be true?'

'I was an eye-witness. Goggle-eyed and petrified, too, I don't mind telling you. Look here, what *is* going on around this coach-station of yours?'

'I wish I knew. Three drivers gone and no knowing when there might have been a fourth, except . . .'

'Except?'

'They've struck. Say it isn't good enough. Say they are not prepared to take any more coaches out until this whole matter is cleared up and the murderer found.'

'Well, I suppose their attitude isn't really surprising, is it?'

'From one point of view perhaps it is not. However, I have one shot left in my locker. I am meeting them tomorrow at eleven and I am going to suggest that I send them out in twos. It means cancelling certain of the tours, of course. I'm working on that at the moment, because I shall try to cancel the least profitable ones and, anyway, the whole thing needs a tremendous amount of reorganisation. There are still a number of coaches out on the road, I'm thankful to say, but unless I can do something to stop the rot, the drivers are going to be got at by these dissidents as soon as the coaches come back, and then the rest of the men will be persuaded to join in the strike.'

'I take it they won't need much persuading.'

'Is Dame Beatrice upset by her dreadful experience?'

'No. I telephoned my husband at headquarters and he is seeing to it that she is under complete protection until Carstairs and Knight are pulled in.'

'Who is Carstairs?'

Laura looked surprised and said:

'A mysterious sort of chap who owns a bungalow on the hillside above the Saighdearan hotel. Nobody seems to know much about him. Apparently he's a bird of passage, sometimes there, but mostly not. It was in his bungalow that Vittorio was found murdered.'

'*What*!'

'I thought you knew. Sorry if I've given you a shock. It's in this morning's paper. I thought you must have seen it.'

'Vittorio murdered? I can't believe it. What on earth was he doing in Saighdearan?'

'Visiting this man Carstairs, apparently. Or, of course,' said Laura, as though she had just been struck by the thought, 'I suppose Vittorio could have been staying with Carstairs. He seems to have been sleeping in Carstairs' bedroom when he was stabbed.'

'Stabbed? Like the other two?'

'Well, yes,' admitted Laura. 'Like them in that only one blow, and that a shrewdly lethal one, seems to have been struck, but, of course, a different weapon may have been used.'

'Did you and Dame Beatrice know about this – this third murder – when I came to lunch?'

'Oh, yes, of course. We knew of it before we left Saighdearan.'

'Yet neither of you mentioned it.'

'The news hadn't been made public, you see. But haven't you looked at your newspaper this morning?'

'I haven't had time. I've been working out these double-driver schedules since before breakfast. I've done nothing but swallow a cup of coffee. I haven't even looked at my correspondence. I suppose I'd better do that.'

'And I'm hindering you,' said Laura. 'Anyway, we thought you'd be interested to hear our news.'

'That somebody broke into the Stone House last night and attempted to murder Dame Beatrice?'

'That's what it looked like to us.'

'God bless my soul!'

'It reminds her, she said, of the editor of that newspaper in the Wild West when some indignant reader tried to shoot him. It meant that he really was getting somewhere with a series of articles he was writing to expose some local racket or other. Dame B feels *she's* getting somewhere over tracking down these murderers. Well, I'd better let you get on.'

'One thing,' said Honfleur, 'we've had lots of cancellations already, so there won't be all that many letters to send out advising people that their tour has been called off. How I do hate paying back all those fares, though. We make them pay us well in advance, you see, so, of course, all that money has to be returned if it's our fault they can't go. As a matter of fact, we refund most of it for any cancellation so long as they give us fair notice that they are not able to make the trip. Goodwill and fair dealing are everything in this game.'

'In every other game, too, one hopes.'

'Yes, of course. Now, Mrs Gavin, what exactly is all this "sweep the dust behind the door" to which you referred?'

'Ah, that, yes. Dame B wants to know whether you are in touch with Conradda Mendel.'

'Conradda? How does *she* come into it?'

'I don't know. Probably she doesn't.'

'I haven't seen or heard of her since that dinner she attended when I entertained Dame Beatrice and Vittorio. You remember?'

'From hearsay, yes.'

'Well, I understood that Conradda had sold her shops and emigrated. That is all I know. To go back to something you mentioned earlier: what did you mean about Carstairs and *Knight* being pulled in? Knight has disappeared, just like Noone and Daigh. Has Dame Beatrice any reason to think that he is still alive?'

'I suppose so. We found no body at Saighdearan except Vittorio's, so she thinks it's possible that Knight is still alive. The police have combed and honeycombed the neighbourhood around Saighdearan, but have found nothing to suggest that he has been murdered — unless he's Vittorio, of course,' Laura added, struck by a sudden idea.

'Quite impossible. I knew them both. They are not in the least alike,' said Honfleur. 'Whatever made you think of that?'

'It was a wild suggestion,' said Laura.

'At any rate, Knight has disappeared,' said Honfleur.

'Yes, he certainly has,' agreed Laura. 'By the way, supposing he turned up again safe and well, would your drivers resume work? That's one of the things I was sent to ask you.'

'But neither you nor Dame Beatrice knew that my drivers were on strike until you came here today.'

Laura wagged her head.

'We didn't *know*,' she admitted, 'but Dame B gave me to understand that it was a fair assumption and, as usual, she turns out to have been right.'

'Well, I hope she's right about Knight, too, and that he'll turn up,' said Honfleur, beginning to fidget with a pencil.

'You want to be busy, I know,' said Laura, 'so I won't keep you any longer. It was a long shot about Conradda, but Dame B thought there was just the chance that you might be in touch with her.'

'Sorry, no.'

Laura took her leave, remarking, as Honfleur opened his office door for her:

'Best of luck in getting your men back to work.'

'I may succeed, if Knight is alive and you can find him for me.'

Laura returned to the Stone House to find Dame Beatrice watched over by a private detective, a retired police-sergeant, whom Laura's husband, in response to an urgent call from his wife, had sent along. Dame Beatrice gravely introduced him to Laura and he retired to the kitchen, leaving them together.

'What news from the Slough of Despond?' she enquired.

'It's that, all right,' said Laura. 'His drivers are going on strike. Could his job be in danger if they do? Apart from that, he knows nothing about Conradda, but Vittorio's death has knocked him all of a heap. He seems to be a very worried man.'

'The loss of three drivers and an impending strike would be quite enough to account for that.'

'I suppose so.'

'There is another factor, too, which may be causing him uneasiness. I have been in touch with one of his directors. It appears that a big merger is on the way. There are four coach-tour companies in the area, one of which is an off-shoot of a very much larger concern based on a Midlands network. It seems that agreement has been reached and that this mammoth concern will take over County Motors after the end of next season.'

'So Honfleur could be made redundant, you think?'

'It is more than possible. These mergers do not tend to improve every employee's position and prospects. Mr Tedworthy, who gave me help over the affair at Hulliwell Hall, is a case in point.'

'I wonder how long Honfleur has known about the merger? He's never mentioned it, has he?'

'Perhaps it is too sore a subject. I wonder how my guardian angel will get on with Henri and Celestine in the kitchen? I deprecate the fact that you have saddled me with an incubus.'

'*I* don't regret it,' said Laura. 'The sound of that thug smashing away at that dummy on your bed will haunt my dreams.'

The crucial days of the following week, so far as Basil Honfleur was concerned, were Saturday, Sunday and Monday, counting Saturday as the first day of the coach-tours week, as the company always did.

Dame Beatrice telephoned from the Stone House on the Friday afternoon at about four to ask how things were going. Honfleur, who had been about to return to his house, was lugubrious.

'I had to talk with the strikers,' he said, 'and got my assistant to waylay every driver as the coaches arrived at the depôt after such tours as had been on the road before all this disaffection got really serious, and I put it to them. Unless the remaining tours were carried out, and the rest of our commitments honoured, I told them, their jobs and their futures were in jeopardy. We are due to be taken over and made part of a huge combine, you know, after the end of next season. I stressed this and promised that County Motors would do their best to protect every man's interests when the take-over came about, but that it was going to be difficult, if not impossible, for me to speak up for men who seemed determined to chuck their jobs away.'

'And what effect did this have?'

'Very little, I'm afraid. There was a lot of muttering and then one chap said that they'd better lose their jobs than their lives, and I could tell that the other fellows agreed with him. This was on Friday. I am calling another meeting at eight on Sunday evening, when the nine-day tours which have been on the road get back, but, frankly, I haven't much hope. The drivers who were supposed to be going up to Scotland tomorrow morning have stuck their feet in and absolutely refused to budge.'

'How many tours does that affect?'

'More than I care to think about. There won't be the Skye tour, or the one which goes up to John o' Groats, Royal Deeside is off and so are the Trossachs, the Ayrshire and Arran tour and the nine-day tour of the Central Highlands. In fact, ironic though it may sound, the only fellow willing to take a coach out at all at present is the driver who takes the party to Swansea to embark on the ferry to Cork, and he is none too keen to do even that much. Even the drivers who do the foreign tours are dragging their feet because they have to take passengers to spend a night in Southampton before crossing to Le Havre. Pusillanimous twits! I only just stopped myself from calling them a bunch of cowards.'

'It might have been injudicious, under the circumstances in which you find yourself, to have called their courage in question. Did you make them the offer you outlined to Laura, that you would send them out in twos?'

'Yes, I did. The trouble is that they no longer trust each other.'

'That is serious. Let us hope for a miracle – in other words, that Driver Knight will turn up safe and sound.'

CHAPTER 13

The Story of a Disappearance

The telephone call had ended with a short, incredulous exclamation from Honfleur, after which he rang off, but on the following morning he rang up the Stone House again. Laura was out for an early morning ride, so Dame Beatrice herself took the call.

'You're not going to believe this,' said the voice at the other end. Dame Beatrice cackled.

'Like the White Queen, I can believe as many as six impossible things before breakfast,' she said, 'and I haven't had breakfast yet.'

'Knight has turned up again, safe and sound.'

'Really? So where has he been all this time?'

'Oh, his story is simple enough. He got a knock on the head and lost his memory.'

'Do you mean somebody attacked him?'

'I suppose you could call it that.'

'Do the Scottish police know that he has reappeared?'

'I've told our own chaps, so I suppose they'll notify Inverness or whoever has to be told.'

'I should like to hear Knight's story.'

'Well, it's going to be a nice day. Why don't you come along? Meet me in my office at ...?'

'Four?'

'Right, I'll have Knight with me and my secretary can make us some tea.'

'Do the other drivers know of Knight's return?'

'Oh, rather! What's more, I was able to persuade them to call off the strike, so although today's coaches won't go out, there shouldn't be any difficulty about tomorrow.'

'They seem to have changed their minds very quickly.'

'Oh, I'm keeping my promise of sending them out in twos. They insist on that.'

'So which tours will go out tomorrow?'

'North Wales, North Devon, St Ives, Llandudno, Yorkshire Wolds, Tenby, Lake District and, of course, our Swiss tour from the airport. It's all perfectly splendid. With the Saturday tours all cancelled for today, I've got plenty of drivers free and by the time the Sunday tours, double-manned, get back and everybody is home and dry, I'm sure our troubles will all be over.'

'It is to be hoped so, but we still haven't found the murderer. Four o'clock in your office, then. I shall be accompanied by Laura and the guardian angel supplied by her husband.'

'What will happen to Knight?' asked Laura when she returned. 'The police will want to question him.'

'Yes, indeed, and from our own point of view it will be very interesting to hear what Driver Knight has to say. I would like you to take his story down word for word and then transcribe it for me. It will make a fascinating study.'

'Because he wasn't murdered, whereas the other two were? He may just have been lucky, don't you think? Anyway, I'm sure he murdered Vittorio.'

'In self-defence, perhaps.'

The interview with Knight took place in Honfleur's office, but Dame Beatrice, her escort, Laura and the driver had it to themselves. Honfleur left a note with his secretary to let Dame Beatrice know that he had been called to a meeting in Bristol with the directors of the firm who were to take over his company. He apologised for his absence, but added that his secretary was fully briefed and would be able to answer any queries which might arise. It was clear, from the young woman's demeanour, that she fully expected to sit in on the interview, but Dame Beatrice decided otherwise and in the most kindly but determined way dispensed with her presence.

'Now, Mr Knight,' she said, when the secretary had left them, 'I am retained, as I expect you know, by your directors, to look into matters which have been troubling the Company since Mr Noone set out for Derbyshire. I am to find out, if I can, why he was murdered and exactly what your own experiences have been.'

'I'm lucky to be alive, I suppose,' said Knight, indicating a bandage round his neck. 'If I hadn't had a Commando training when I was a young fellow, I might not be as tough as I am. Comes back to you, you know, when you find yourself in a tight spot. More than thirty years since I was demobbed, but I'm as fit as ever I was, and a good thing, too, I reckon.'

'I shall be glad of a full account. You say you are as fit as ever you were, but I understand that you had been ill and away from work before you took this coach up to Scotland.'

'First time ever, but sooner or later the job finds you out. I got a spot of gastric trouble and had to lie up for a week or two, that's all. Didn't ought to have come back as soon as I did, but one of my mates told me how short-handed Mr Honfleur was, with Noone and Daigh gone missing, so I reckoned I'd better help out.'

'Very self-sacrificing, and your only reward was to get knocked on the head, I am told; and your neck, I see, is bandaged. But please begin at the beginning. I have had an account of the tour from a passenger, but your own story will be a great deal more valuable, as you seem to have been the victim of a most unpleasant and, I daresay, alarming experience.'

'You want me to start . . .'

'From the time your coach moved off from the depôt, if you will be so good.'

'I see the young lady is taking notes.'

'She will read them back to you later on, if you wish.'

'Like a bloomin' police station, isn't it? Oh, well, I've got nothing to hide. I reported for duty as usual on the Saturday morning and I'm told it's the Skye tour as I'm to take on. I wasn't too keen, having done Scotland previous only as far as Edinburgh except once, and then a different schedule – the Trossachs and that – but I'd said I'd muck in, whatever Mr Honfleur wanted me to do, so I showed willing, as they say, and we got the luggage stowed and the first few passengers aboard and off we went, only about eight minutes behind time. Wouldn't have been that, only two people coming by car were involved in a collision and had to come on by taxi. A bit shaken up they were, too, and not at all sure whether they wanted to make the tour or not, but our inspector cheered them up and they came. Silly not to, when they'd paid their money.

'Well, I picked up a couple of people here and another one or two there, along the route, you know, but the main lot joined us in Canonbury. That bus station needs enlarging or else to be taken right out of the town. Still, that's by the way and just my usual bit of bellyache.

'We made the lunch stop all right and later on I allowed twenty minutes for tea. I got the coach in at six for dinner and the night. No problems; passengers a quiet lot, coach running sweet, everybody happy.'

'Where was that first overnight stop?'

'Where was our first overnight stop? Oh, in Yorkshire at Harrogate. One of our favourite hotels. Very popular with the coach parties because not only is it well situated – close to the park and all that – but the accommodation and food are very high-class, and a lot of camera-clicking goes on because the coach is always met by a chap dressed in the old horse-coach rig-out and he blows a coach-horn to welcome the visitors. We only stayed there the one night, and then we went on to Edinburgh by way of Newcastle and Carter Bar and, the old bus running like a song, we fetched up in fine weather at the overnight stop at just after six. Everybody pleased with the hotel, Princes Street crowded and the traffic non-stop as usual, and then we set off in the rain next morning, and me with no experience of the route once we'd crossed the Forth Bridge.'

'But you had been to Saighdearan once before and you were able to give two of your party the names of the mountains they saw when the coach stopped for lunch on the shores of, I think, Loch Earn.'

'Oh, Lord, yes, I forgot my first trip that way. Anyhow, I'd done my homework the night before. Always reckon to do that, you know. Never like to plead ignorant. Matter of professional pride, I suppose. Anything more you want to know about the trip?'

He sounded jaunty and cocksure, but Dame Beatrice knew that he was uneasy and that his further account of the tour might be only partly true.

'Nothing more about the tour,' she said, 'but I should like as clear and as detailed a description as possible of what happened after the party had returned from the day's outing to Skye.'

'Oh, ah, Skye. We had to wait a bit at Kyle of Lochalsh for the bigger boat to take the coach, you know. The trip passed off all right, although people would have liked to see a lot more of Skye than we had time for, and then —'

'When you got back you were attacked?'

'Yes, that was all of a rum go, that was. I thought my number was up, and that's a fact. Third time unlucky, I guessed.'

'Third time?'

'Well, Noone and Daigh, you know. Both copped it, didn't they? So when these two blokes broke into my bedroom just as I'd settled down to bone up on the next day's run from Fort William to Perth, I reckoned I'd had it, just like the other two.'

'Can you describe the men?'

'Not really. They had nylon stockings over their heads. One I reckon was a spade.'

'A black man?'

'That's right. They both were wearing gloves, but I caught a sight of a bit of bare brown wrist while they were gagging me and tying me up.'

'Did you have no chance to raise the alarm?'

'No chance at all. They come busting in and were on me and the gag in my mouth before I could let out a single, solitary yip.'

'Were you fully dressed?'

'What's that got to do with it? Matter of fact, I was in trousers and shirt and my dressing-gown.'

'Had you left your bedroom door open?'

'No, of course not. One of them must have been on the staff of the hotel, I reckon, because he must have had a master-key to the rooms.'

'Could you not have called out while they were stripping off your dressing-gown?'

'Stripping off my dressing-gown? Look here, madam, what are you getting at?'

'Oh, I took it for granted that they would have seen to it that you were fully dressed when they spirited you away. Tell me about that.'

'I want to know what my dressing-gown has to do with it.'

'I have told you.'

'You haven't the right to question me like this. All I've got to say I've said to the police.'

'Very well. By the way, are you preparing to ask for compensation?'

'Compensation?'

'I have no authority to make promises on behalf of County Motors, of course, but it seems, from your story (and I do hope you will be good enough to continue it), that you have suffered physical injury and, I assume, unlawful captivity while employed upon the Company's business.'

'Oh, I see. Well, Mr Honfleur is a decent chap, so he'll see I
get my rights. As for unlawful captivity, well, you can say that
again. They sat there in the room, me trussed up like a chicken
ready for the oven excepting that I'd still got my guts inside me,
although my heart, I don't mind telling you, was just about in
my boots, and then, when it was dark, which comes latish, as
you may have noticed, as far north as that, they forced me, at
knife-point, to get down the stairs and out into the open.'

'So they had not tied your legs?'

'They did, until they were ready for us to leave. Then this
darkie pulled out a dirty great flick-knife and stood behind me
and reached round and put it at my throat while the other chap
untied my legs and told me to get moving. I had a shot at grab-
bing the darkie's wrist and got this nasty snick on my neck.'

'Your bedroom was in the three-storey wing, then.'

'Yes, right at the top. I don't think any of my passengers were
near me. I believe they were all on the ground floor in the
bungalow part of the building. Still, even if any of them had been
handy, I wouldn't have cared to risk a shout.'

'And, in any case, you were gagged, you say. So you emerged
into the front yard of the hotel. What happened then?'

'They forced me into a car and drove me a few hundred yards
down the road in the direction of Fort William. They took me
into a big, empty house which looked about ready to fall down
and kept me there.'

'And, later, released you.'

'That's right, in a sense, I suppose.'

'Did they feed you?'

'Yes, with sandwiches from the lorry-drivers' caff down the
road and tea out of a thermos.'

'What demands did they make?'

'Demands? Nothing, except to tell them the exact route the
coaches take to get back home from Perth. Well, there was no
secret about that, so I told them. When I'd done and had
answered several questions about the hotels we were ac-

customed to stop at, the nig hit me over the head and the next thing I knew I was walking into Mr Honfleur's office here.'

'With no idea of how you got back from Saighdearan?'

'I suppose I must have thumbed lifts, but I've no recollection of it.'

'But your memory has returned to you?'

'Except for what happened between the knock on the head and me walking in on Mr Honfleur yesterday afternoon.'

'What an interesting story! And you have no idea why you were abducted in this strange fashion?'

'None at all.'

'But you were able to leave this tumbledown house of your own volition.'

'I must have, mustn't I? But I can't remember a thing about it.'

'And there was no sign of these men?'

'Neither hair nor hide.'

'They had untied you, I assume.'

'Must have done, mustn't they?'

'While you were at Saighdearan did you make contact with a man named Vittorio?'

'Make contact? Me? No. Why should I?' (But the question had rattled him.)

'Only because I have some reason to believe that he was in the neighbourhood at the same time as you were. You know him, of course?'

'Not to say know him. He came on my coach a year or two back to buy up some antiques or something of that sort, and I believe he used to go along with other drivers from time to time on the same sort of job, but I haven't seen him around for a year or more.'

'It's all right,' said Laura. 'I was not going to read out my shorthand notes in front of Knight. He might have started thinking about his dressing-gown, which we happen to know was neatly packed and stowed away in his suitcase.'

'His kidnappers may have tidy minds.'

'The man is a liar of liars. His whole story is a fabrication and not a very clever one at that. All that boloney about a black man!'

'The boy at the hotel mentioned a black man.'

'Yes, but he meant Vittorio.'

'I have suggested that to the police. No doubt they will have confirmed it by now.'

'And Knight's loss of memory which he claims happened after he was knocked on the head! What do you think he was up to during his so-called disappearance?'

'Murdering Vittorio.'

'Then he *must* be Carstairs!'

'We have already decided that point, I think.'

'Look, though, are we *sure* that Knight and Carstairs are not the same man? It would simplify things enormously if they were.'

'No, no. Things are simple enough. The jigsaw is not a difficult one. It only remains for us to fit the pieces together in a manner which will convince a jury and that, at the moment, we are not in a position to do.'

'You mean you know all the answers?'

'So would you, if you would rid yourself of this yearning for Carstairs and Knight to be one and the same man. What about the descriptions we have had of both? We must accept evidence when it is provided by unbiased witnesses. I think there is no doubt, as you say, that Knight's story is a fabrication, except in so far as the wound in his neck is concerned. I made him take the bandage off, as you know. The snick is neither deep nor dangerous, but it must have bled fairly considerably when it was inflicted.'

'Yes, but by whom? Carstairs?'

'Vittorio, I think, and then Knight killed him.'

'So we are going on the assumption that Knight murdered

Vittorio. But that looks as though Vittorio knew that Knight had murdered Noone and Daigh, doesn't it?'

'Oh, not necessarily at all. To my mind it does not follow.'

'But Knight has told us all those lies. Do you think he told Basil Honfleur the same story as he told us?'

'Oh, probably. I would not call Knight a very inventive man.'

'You don't believe Knight killed the other two drivers, but you *do* think he murdered Vittorio. Why?'

'Let us say that our jigsaw contains some extraneous pieces and that now we have to select the one piece which fits.'

CHAPTER 14

Conradda Mendel Speaks

'So what's the next move? Are you going to get the Scottish police to check Knight's story?' asked Laura.

'They will do that without any hint from me, but I doubt whether they will be able to disprove it.'

'It's said that a negative is the most difficult thing in the world to prove. I mean, nobody at the hotel can say that Knight wasn't gagged, bound and threatened with a flick-knife, and the fact that the hotel has four exits can't be gainsaid. Besides that, the door by which he says he and those men left is at the foot of the stairs and under no supervision whatever. That's another point in his favour, and I bet the police find plenty of faked evidence in that old house to show that Knight was dumped there. There will be a length of rope, plenty of crumbs and a thermos flask with his fingerprints on it, don't you think?'

'It is not at all unlikely.'

'The police will spot that his story about being in his dressing-gown is phoney, won't they, though?'

'If he is pressed he will tell them that the men put him into his jacket and returned the dressing-gown to his suitcase. He will continue to plead loss of memory.'

'What about his knowing that Daigh, as well as Noone , has been murdered? That news was carefully kept out of the papers until quite recently.'

'He will say that the other drivers told him that Daigh had not returned to the depôt and that another driver brought Daigh's coach home. He will claim that, as he knew Noone had been murdered, he supposed that Daigh had met with a similar fate.'

'Got it all taped out, haven't you?'

'Oh, you are not the only innocent person who has a criminal's mind,' said Dame Beatrice. 'There is one thing I should like to know, though. In the beginning, when the directors of County Motors asked me to look into the matter of the missing coach-drivers, I felt that Basil Honfleur was not at all anxious that I should. When *Knight* was thought to have disappeared, however, who so anxious that I should search for him as our friend Honfleur, and I have found myself wondering how long he has known about this coming merger with the larger coach company and to what extent he fears for his position as managing director when the merger takes place, that is all. As we said before, he would not be the first man in an executive position to be made redundant.'

'So you think he's made himself a little escape route? But how?'

'I do not know, but, as Mrs George de Horne Vaizey, of whom you have never heard, once said, "Human nature is desperately wicked." '

'What was she talking about?'

'Strawberries and cream.'

Laura, who did not trust her employer's sense of humour, snorted disgustedly and changed the subject.

'Wonder how Conradda Mendel is getting on, now she's been mentioned,' she said. As though she had invoked the spirit of the woman in question, on the following morning a letter arrived from Conradda herself.

'So she didn't go to America after all,' Laura remarked as she sorted the correspondence and noted the postmark.

'Who?' Dame Beatrice enquired.

'Conradda Mendel. She's put her name, but not her address,

on the back of the envelope and it's postmarked *Poole* on the front.'

'Interesting. Let us see what she has to say.' Dame Beatrice slit open the envelope, scanned its contents and then handed the missive to Laura.

'Dear Friend,' Conradda had written, 'before I go further, please do not show this to anybody but your most confidential secretary, as I do not wish it to be known to any but yourselves where I am to be found.

'I became ill in America, but it is too expensive to be ill in that country, so I dragged myself on to an aeroplane and came to my own doctor and he ordered an operation, so here I am in convalescence in the house of a friend. I am getting stronger every day, but am not very well yet, so this is to ask if you will kindly visit me, as at the moment I am not able to travel to visit you.

'Now it is about this coach-driver whose body was found in such a strange situation, and I am troubling myself in my mind that he may not be the only one.'

'Well, he isn't,' said Laura, looking up from the letter. 'Shall you go and see her?'

'Read to the end. You will find that I have very little option.'

'You will remember,' the letter went on, 'my telling you of the treasures of Chinese art which Vittorio showed me when I visited his lodging and of the conclusion I reached regarding this surprising and very valuable collection. I also mentioned, I believe, some jade that he had there. Well, jade is always nice; nice material and very patient carving is necessary and takes much time. The pieces he showed me, though, were not very special – jewellers' pieces I would call them – and some were soapstone, not jade.

'Mind, I did not let Vittorio know I recognised some of the china he showed me. That perhaps would not have been a safe thing to do; neither, naturally, did I intend to tell him I should advise you not to buy, but, with much caution, I began to make enquiries about him in the trade and some strange things came out.

'Where County Motors go there are thefts of art treasures. Nobody makes the connection, I think, but me. Now here, now there, I hear of these thefts and because I know Vittorio and your Mr Honfleur are in collusion for Vittorio to purchase antiques —'

'*Our* Mr Honfleur indeed!' said Laura indignantly. 'I like her cheek!'

'She means no harm. Read to the end.'

'. . . to purchase antiques, I ask myself whether this is coincidence or not. I check up the coach tours and it looks less and less like coincidence and more and more like something arranged. You see, my dear friend, when there is a theft the police are told. They cordon off roads and stop cars and perhaps lorries; but who ever heard of police stopping a holiday coach? Even if they did, what would they find? Thirty suitcases of innocent people; souvenirs bought to take home as gifts for friends or as reminders of the holiday; parcels, coats, anoraks and mackintoshes on the racks; everybody able to account for himself. All the same, I think to myself that there may also be one suitcase too many in the boot of the coach. You understand me?

'But the police do not stop the coaches. In most cases they do not stop the cars either. And why? Because, by the time the thefts are discovered and reported, it is too late. The thieves have got clean away and the coach is staying, so innocently, at a hotel in another county, so nobody gives it a thought that there are stolen antiques on board.'

'I wonder whether she's right?' said Laura, handing back the letter. 'It sounds a bit too easy to me. Do you think she's romancing?'

'That is what I propose to find out.'

'Do I go with you to Poole?'

'Yes, I shall need you to take notes. We know already that Vittorio used to take these coach tours. The reason given to us was that he looked out for antiques to sell to Basil Honfleur for his collection of ceramics.'

'Can't quarrel with that, can we?'

'On the face of it, no, except that Honfleur's collection seemed rather too small to account for these elaborate journeys. Of course it could be that Honfleur was not the only collector on Vittorio's list of customers. However, we may know more when we hear what Conradda Mendel has to tell us when we visit her.'

'Considering that there's already been an attempt on your life, I'm not so keen on this visit. Supposing Conradda is in cahoots with Knight and this letter is a trap?'

'I shall look to you to protect me.'

'I might not be able to protect you from a stab in the back. Vittorio was not the only person to be far too handy with a dagger, as witness his own demise, and, if I know anything of the address on Conradda's letter, Poole harbour might be a nice handy dumping-place for a dead body.'

'You make my blood run cold.'

'Not half as much as you make mine curdle in my veins. Look here, how much do we really know about Conradda? Nothing, except that she was a patient of yours. People who need help from a psychiatrist are not always the most trustworthy of friends.'

'You malign my profession and my clients, and in the same breath, too.'

'Would you like to make me feel a lot happier?'

'Your happiness is my chief concern.'

'Right – although I know that was said tongue in cheek, I want our private dick to go with us to Poole. I don't like this sudden summons from Conradda. We don't know for certain that she ever went to America and we *do* know she had that peculiar link-up with Vittorio.'

Laura, who had often had a boat out on Poole harbour, knew the neighbourhood well and was not mistaken in her idea that the house at which Conradda was staying would be in the oldest part of the town and near the quay. It was in a narrow street behind the Customs House and could have done with a coat of paint. All the same, the steps had been cleaned and the brass knocker in the shape of the Three Wise Monkeys had been lovingly polished until it glittered in the sunshine.

The door was opened by a woman wearing a black shawl over a blue overall. She did not ask their names, but invited the visitors in to a linoleum-covered hall which contained a coat-and-umbrella stand and a grandfather clock, and said,

'I'll just pop up and see whether she's awake.' Before she could mount the narrow staircase, however, a voice from the top of it called out:

'Come right up, Dame Beatrice. I saw your car pull in to the kerb.'

'It's a bed-sitter,' said the woman, 'so I don't know about the gentleman without he's a relation, because likely she'll be in bed.'

'Of course he'll come up with us,' said Laura curtly. Conradda was not in bed. The bed, in fact, was a studio couch and had been converted to its daytime use as a settee. Conradda looked pale and puffy. There was little doubt that she had been ill. She seemed delighted to see Dame Beatrice, who reminded her that she had met Laura at the Stone House when she had been under treatment there. Then she introduced the private detective, not as such, but simply as Richard Ross.

'Well, ladies,' said Ross, having decided that the apartment contained no nefarious characters, 'perhaps I could have a smoke out on the landing.'

'Oh, please, yes. Take a chair with you and here is an ashtray,' said Conradda, eagerly embracing this suggestion.

'And please stay close outside the door,' muttered Laura in the detective's ear, as she ushered out him and his chair. As soon as the door had closed behind him, Dame Beatrice said:

'We take Ross everywhere since an attempt was made upon my life a few days ago.'

'An attempt on your life? Oh, but no!' cried Conradda, horrified.

'No doubt about it at all,' said Laura, 'so we take what precautions we can. After all, three men have been stabbed to death and somebody seemed quite determined to lay out Dame B.'

'*Three* men?'

'Yes. The man we knew as Vittorio was the third,' explained Dame Beatrice. 'It happened in Scotland in a tiny place just outside Fort William. But we mustn't tire you with too much talking. Tell us why you sent for me.'

'Ah, yes, you will be wondering about that. But first – this man Vittorio. Is it known who killed him?'

'There are two known suspects; the driver Knight tells a strange story about having been assaulted and kidnapped, and then there is a man called Carstairs who has a bungalow very close to the hotel where Knight claims that he was surprised and captured, and it was in this bungalow that Vittorio was stabbed to death.'

'You think this Knight and this Carstairs are the same person?'

'It would be such a help, I feel, if they were, but we have seen Knight and from the descriptions we have received of Carstairs from independent and presumably unbiased witnesses it does not seem as though Carstairs and Knight can possibly be the same man.'

'I see. It is a gang and, of course, they are smugglers. They smuggle stolen antiques from here to Ireland and from Ireland to America.'

'So we have thought. What do you know about it?'

'Now that Vittorio is dead, perhaps what I have to tell you is not so important as I thought. Does anyone know you have come here to visit me?'

'Only the man outside the door.'

'You see, I do not like all these killings.'

'Does anybody? Please go on.'

'This begins with what I told you before. You remember I go to Vittorio's lodging and see this stuff that I am sure is stolen?'

'Yes, I remember it clearly.'

'Well, a month or more goes by and I conduct my business as usual and think no more of what I have seen and then one day this Honfleur, with whom we have dined, comes into my shop very much upset and asks can he speak to me privately on a matter of great importance. Well, of course, I know of the connection between him and Vittorio, how Vittorio finds him good pieces at a nice price and I think I see how the land lies. Honfleur, I think to myself, is stuck with some stolen pieces which Vittorio obtains for him and now he finds out they are stolen and wants to know what to do. He has paid good money for them, so naturally he does not want to give them up, and yet he knows that, if the police trace them to his house, not only will they be confiscated but he may find himself in big trouble as well for harbouring stolen property.'

'It was a very intelligent guess on your part,' said Dame Beatrice.

'Not so intelligent, no, because it is much worse than I think. It is not advice this Honfleur wants, but for me to hide his stolen goods while he thinks what to do.'

'Of course you refused.'

'At first, yes, but there is more. He tells me that Vittorio blackmails him. He says that Vittorio wishes him to buy the things I describe to you – all that beautiful stuff of Chinese art, best periods – and tells him that if he do not, Vittorio will rat on him to the police that he has other stolen property in his possession.'

'And had he?'

'Oh, yes, of course,' said Conradda, as though the question surprised her. 'This Honfleur do not know how much I know about him, but perhaps you remember that, before we leave to go home, I retire upstairs for usual reasons? Well, I do a quick snoop around up there and I recognise one or two things.'

'What made you think of doing a quick snoop around?' asked Laura, fascinated by a mentality so alien from and yet so sympathetic to her own.

'Simple. I am not satisfied by that Welsh dresser.'

'It looked all right to me.'

'The dresser, yes. The contents, no. What are we shown? Some good pieces, yes, but on the shelves where everybody may see. Nothing of value in the drawers and cupboards, no good pictures on the walls, nothing but those pretty but silly little carved spoons which Vittorio himself repudiates and which Honfleur let Dame Beatrice have in return for her platters with no haggling, no bargaining, no fun at all.'

'I don't see what in this aroused your suspicions,' said Laura. 'The English are not very good at that sort of thing. Dame B would think it beneath her dignity to haggle. She would either buy or refuse to buy, and that would be that.'

'I understand, but I deprecate. Not so is trade carried on. But you talk of my suspicions and you do not approve when I make an excuse to go upstairs and take opportunity to case the joint. Why not?'

'Oh, please don't think I'm blaming you, but exactly *why* did you snoop?'

'Because if, as we are told by Honfleur, this Vittorio find him nice stuff at a good price, where is the rest of it and why are we not shown? Mind, at that time, I do not know this Vittorio, but my instincts tell me not to trust him. He is – how shall I put it?'

'A greasy bird,' suggested Laura, quoting.

'That is very good. A greasy bird. We meet them all the time in my business, you know. Well, of course I have to be quick, but in the bedroom I have time to spot some nice things, many of them on the police list.'

'Are you sure about that?' asked Dame Beatrice.

'Oh, quite sure. There are pictures of which I know their homes; ceramics much, much better than some we are shown on the dresser; in a cabinet a collection of snuff-boxes of which, even at a glance, I recognise two or three. Oh, and you remember I said Vittorio's jade and soapstone does not interest me? But in this Honfleur's bedroom! Museum pieces! Beautiful! Priceless! And all stolen. I am sure of it. It is a marvellous collection and I wish I dare look further around in other rooms, but there is no time.'

'And then Vittorio invited you to go with him to see his Chinese collection.'

'So. Well, of course, when I get back to my hotel I am deep in thought. Why, I ask myself, does this Vittorio invite me? Does he know, after all, that I am expert in ceramics? I cannot answer myself. Maybe it is as he says. He wishes me to interest Dame Beatrice. So I warn Dame Beatrice and then I put it all out of my mind and carry on my business as usual until this Honfleur come to my London shop.'

'Ah! said Laura. 'And here *we* come to the point!'

'Oh, no. The point has been made, I think,' said Dame Beatrice. 'The point is blackmail, as Conradda has indicated.'

Conradda spread her hands.

'This Honfleur comes to my shop in London a second time,' she said, 'and asks for another interview in private. I am not at all keen on this. I think perhaps he wishes this time to sell some of his stolen goods to me, and so it is. It turns out that Vittorio puts more pressure on Honfleur to buy the Chinese ceramics. Honfleur says only too pleased if the price is right. He has told Vittorio this many times before, but the price is never right.'

'So, in the end, Vittorio told Honfleur, I suppose, that if he did not buy the ceramics at Vittorio's price, he would inform upon Honfleur as a receiver of stolen goods.'

'That is so, of course, but Honfleur this time simply asks me to buy his collection of jade so he can get enough money to pay Vittorio for the ceramics, which he confesses he knows were stolen.'

'But you, believing the jade to have been stolen, too, very

properly refused any part in the transaction.'

'Of course, yes. Honfleur goes away very sad, very worried. In no way, he tells me, can he find the money Vittorio asks unless he can sell other things. He offers me snuff-boxes — well, but I have seen one in his room which I know I have seen in a ducal mansion and which has been in the police list, so I say *no* to the snuff-boxes. Then I say *no* when he offers me a Picasso, and again *no* to a pair of gold-inlaid pistols which I have not spotted in his house but which he describes as the work of the gun-maker to King William the Third.'

'Aha!' exclaimed Laura. Conradda glanced at her, but went on:

'So, like I am saying, Honfleur goes away sad. Then comes this snake Vittorio and offers *me* again to buy the china. I say no sale for such important stuff among my clients, so no reason to buy. So he say he will inform on me that I have the Ming and the Sung and the K'ang Hsi pottery and all the rest of it in my basement. Of course I say this is nonsense, but he says that when he tip off the police it will not be nonsense.'

'He was going to plant it on you?' asked Laura.

'So. Well, I am alarmed. The police I fear very much because of my life in Nazi Germany. So I pretend to capitulate. I stall. I say I need to find the money and then a buyer. I say maybe I sell my smaller shop. He agrees three months for this, so I sell both my shops and fly to America, and now you bring me good news to tell me he is dead.'

'But why did you send for me?' asked Dame Beatrice. '*I* told Honfleur the Chinese stuff was stolen.'

'To ask you to help me if Vittorio ever find out where I am living now. I was afraid of him, but now — no more!'

CHAPTER 15

So Does Basil Honfleur

'Well, that was a tale and a half, if you like!' said Laura, when, leaving a greatly comforted Conradda, they were on their way home. 'How much of it was moonshine, do you suppose?'

'We may find that out when we have had another talk with Basil Honfleur.'

'Yes. If what Conradda says is true, Honfleur certainly had not finished with Vittorio when he told us he had sacked him.'

'Let us examine her story and see exactly what she has told us.'

'It hasn't helped much, has it?'

'Well, as you point out, if what she said is true, it does not look as though Basil Honfleur has been entirely frank with us.'

'And you think he's been in cahoots all the time with Vittorio over this thieving and smuggling racket. In other words, he has never been the innocent party he pretends to be. Even allowing fot the fact that he may be going to lose his job when this merger takes place, it hardly seems worth the risk, especially as it put him in Vittorio's power.'

'People have different ways of looking at these things. As for Conradda, well, it appeared that she knew nothing of Vittorio's death.'

'It's not important either way, is it?'

'Not unless she killed him.'

165

'Oh, not any red herrings, *please!*'

'I apologise. Next, Conradda stated very definitely that she knows a gang of thieves and smugglers have been in operation and that the stolen antiques are sent to Ireland and on to America.'

'Means the thieves must have clients over there who are willing to buy as soon as the stuff is landed.'

'Yes, that much is clear. Then she told us that Honfleur visited her — and this is where I find her story difficult to credit — and asked her to hide his stolen property. That, I think, was a lie.'

'Very hard to swallow, certainly. I thought so at the time she said it.'

'She has a devious mind. Then she went on to tell us what is much more likely to be the truth.'

'That Honfleur tried to flog her some of his hot merchandise. The question, I suppose, is whether he knew it was hot when he bought first of all from Vittorio. After that, of course, he was completely trapped and had to carry on. So we tackle Honfleur again and push him hard, I take it.'

'That depends upon how the interview goes. At any rate it should be an interesting one. Have you ever wondered why the drivers Noone and Daigh were murdered?'

'I thought that's what we've been wondering ever since the board of directors called you in to investigate their disappearance. It seems clear enough, I think, that they must have got wind of the thieving and smuggling, kicked up about it, or, at any rate, refused to co-operate, and so had to be liquidated because they knew too much and were honest men. Isn't that the way you see it? That makes it all the more certain, to my mind, that Knight was implicated, otherwise he'd have been killed as well. Do you think Knight carried out the murders and not Vittorio?'

'I do not think it was Knight who hit upon the hiding-places for the bodies.'

'But it *was* Knight who murdered Vittorio, wasn't it?'

'Well, thieves have fallen out before now. What intrigues me is that the scene of operations shifted to Scotland as soon as Knight reported for duty at the end of his so-called sick-leave. I am also interested in the fact that his disappearance lasted such a comparatively short time.'

'What do you deduce from that?'

'Only that it was unnecessary for him to disappear for a longer period,' said Dame Beatrice, leering aggravatingly at her secretary. 'It all begins to fall into place rather nicely,' she added. 'And now for Basil Honfleur.'

'You think he's Carstairs, don't you?' said Laura suddenly. Dame Beatrice surveyed her with admiration and amusement.

'I have never had much doubt about that,' she said.

'Then – then ...' said Laura.

'Yes, you are right about that, too,' Dame Beatrice assured her, but without mentioning the subject about which Laura had guessed correctly.

'One thing occurs to me,' said Dame Beatrice when she and Laura and the bodyguard were seated in Honfleur's office, 'and that is the recollection of a sentence in your letter which resulted in Conradda Mendel's visit to you when you invited us to dinner.'

'Oh, yes? I don't remember putting anything of importance in the letter.' He shifted his position in his chair.

'You do not remember specifying that I should bring with me somebody who had an interest in ceramics?'

'Oh, that! What of it? It was only because I thought it only fair that Vittorio should have an opponent when it came to putting a value on those delftware dishes I suggested you should bring with you.'

'So Vittorio guessed, if he did not already know, that Miss Mendel was an expert in that field, did he not?'

'I haven't the faintest idea.'

'Well, but, immediately the visit was over, Vittorio persuaded

Miss Mendel to go with him to his lodging so that she could inspect a very valuable collection of Chinese pottery.'

'I see nothing significant in that.'

'Subsequently you yourself called at her London shop and put
two rather extraordinary suggestions to her.'

'Good Lord!' said Honfleur, with an unconvincing shout of
laughter. 'You make me sound like Casanova!'

'Such was not my intention. First you made the strange
suggestion that she should hide some property for you —'

'I never did!'

'Which you either knew or suspected had been stolen —'

'Never! Who's been telling these lies?' There was no doubt
about his discomfiture.

'And when, very sensibly, she refused, as you must have
known she would, you then tried to sell her some of the stolen
goods. Jade carvings and jewelled snuff-boxes were mentioned, I
believe. At this, she became so much alarmed that she sold up
her businesses and fled to America, where, I presume, she has
friends.'

'This is all moonshine, you know. I mean, whether she sold up
and went to America is beside the point. For all I know, she
herself may have been a receiver of stolen goods and was afraid
the police were after her. Nothing would surprise me less, but to
suggest that *I* had anything to do with any doubtful transactions
is not only derisible, it's actionable and I don't advise you to
repeat it.'

'Your advice comes a little late in the day.'

'What! You don't mean you *have* repeated it? If you have, I'll
sue you.'

'Why not sue the police while you are about it? Sit down and
refrain from agitation. We know all about Mr Carstairs, I may
tell you.'

'Carstairs? I don't know what you're talking about!' It was a
bold attempt at bluster, but Honfleur's cheeks had fallen in, his
lips were trembling and his tell-tale hands were being clasped

and unclasped in the agitation against which Dame Beatrice had advised him.

'While we have been talking,' she said, 'my guardian angel, from his modest seat near the door, has taken one or two photographs of you. The light is excellent in here. When these photographs are shown to Mr and Mrs MacGregor White, Carstairs' next-door neighbours, I have no doubt they will recognise an acquaintance who sometimes is at Saighdearan and sometimes – possibly more often – is not.'

'Look,' said Honfleur, after a long pause during which Dame Beatrice regarded him with the bright gaze of a bird waiting for a worm, 'I'd better tell you all about it. One thing I swear. I swear it on my soul.'

'A doubtful commodity, but pray continue. What do you swear? – that you had nothing to do with the three murders which have taken place since you became embroiled with these nefarious characters?'

'That's it. You must believe me. After all, why would I kill my own drivers?'

'With your own job in jeopardy, why should you care what happened to your drivers?'

'You're heartless and cruel!'

'So was the person who killed Noone and Daigh, but please proceed, remembering, if you are wise, that I am in a position to check some part, if not the whole, of your story.'

'It began,' said Honfleur miserably, 'when I first made Vittorio's acquaintance. I believe he booked with us first as an ordinary passenger. I can't remember which tour it was – one of those which does the Yorkshire dales, I believe – and a day or two after it returned he called here at my office and said that he wished to make a personal complaint. That is how I came to know him.

'I told him he must make it in writing. I said that dealing with complaints was not part of my job. "You must write to the company," I told him. "I am only responsible for checking on the bookings, arranging and sometimes changing the hotels, and looking after the welfare of the personnnel."

'Well, he grinned in a nasty sort of way and picked up the word. "Ah, yes, the personnel," he said. "I think, *signore,* you had better listen to what I have to tell you." This sounded a bit sinister, so I gave him a chair, sent for my secretary as a witness and invited him to go ahead.

'He started to tell me some garbled story about the coach-driver and one of the women passengers, but I soon cut him short. "Look here," I said, "if the lady has been assaulted or in any way annoyed, it is up to her to complain. We may assume that she hasn't complained. My directors would soon have taken action if she had, I do assure you. The coach-driver," I said, "has a position of being *in loco parentis* to his passengers. He is not a chap out on the spree doing a gay Lothario act. If the lady hasn't complained, either what you have told me is entirely false and a figment of your prurient imagination, or else," I said, "she was a willing participant in whatever went on. In that case there is no more to be said. Had she been your wife," I said, "You might well have cause for complaint. As it is, you have none. And what were you yourself doing, prowling about hotel corridors when you should have been in bed and asleep?"

'He said he had had occasion to get up for the usual reason. I said, "What! With a bathroom to every bedroom? You seem to forget I know all our hotels and what the amenities are." '

'That shook him, I'll bet!' said Laura. 'Do you like "amenities" spelt with one *m* or two? – not that it will make any difference until I type out my shorthand.'

Dame Beatrice wagged her head at Laura in a reproving manner and said to Honfleur,

'And that remark of yours terminated the interview, I take it?'

'Well, it did, in one sense, but, in another sense, it didn't. He said he had only been testing me. "That's like your damn' cheek!" I said. "Get out of here before I kick you out."

' "No, honestly," he said, "I've been sent here for that very purpose, to try you out. We just wanted to know what sort of fellow you were, and whether you were prepared to back up your office staff and go bail for your drivers and all that."

' "What the hell do you mean by 'we'?" I said; but I don't mind telling you, Dame Beatrice, that I was worried. You see, quite by accident I had been given access to certain papers which were supposed at the time to be strictly confidential . . .'

'About the projected merger between your own County Motors and a very much larger organisation?'

'Yes, that's it. How Vittorio had found out anything about it I have no idea. Somebody blabbed while under the influence, I imagine, and Vittorio, who was never anybody's fool, picked it up as it came off the bat, I suppose.'

'But such information (if, at that time, as you indicate, it had not been released) could only have been known at top level. Vittorio did not strike me as a man who would be on drinking terms with tycoons,' said Dame Beatrice.

'I don't suppose I was the only person who collected antiques, and that, as you know, was his line.'

'I understand. Neither were you the only one of his clients who liked to pay a low price for stolen goods, I think.'

'Strawberries and cream,' said Laura. Dame Beatrice cackled. Honfleur looked puzzled and anxious. His flash of belligerence had gone.

'So you believed at the time that, as Vittorio was in possession of this so-far exclusive information about the merger, he must be what he claimed to be – the accredited representative of the firm into which County Motors was to be absorbed. I suppose,' said Dame Beatrice. 'That was his story, was it not?'

'That's the size of it,' said Honfleur, relieved. 'Well, of course, as soon as I found out about the merger I realised that my own job might be at stake, so when Vittorio invited me out for a drink, I thought that, as he was evidently top brass in the other coach company, it might be politic to play ball with him, so I went along.

'We chatted over our drinks (which he paid for) and, of course, it came out that I had already known about the merger.'

'And at that point *he* came out in his true colours, no doubt.'

'You're dead right he did. He told me that the merger was supposed to be top secret and that unless I played along with him he would blow the gaff to my board of directors. "And if I do that," he said, "you won't have to worry whether your job is going to be safe or not, will you? – because there won't be any job for you to worry about. Leakage of confidential information is a serious matter, isn't it?"

'Well, I was still believing that he really *was* a key man in the other company, so I said I'd only come upon my information by accident and never intended to make use of it. I said I didn't see how I *could* make use of it, even if I wanted to, which I most certainly did not. He laughed at me.

' "Yours isn't the only coach company in this take-over business," he said. "What's to stop me leaking the information to some of the others, using your name, eh? That would put the cat among the pigeons, wouldn't it?"

' "I should deny it and denounce you to your own company," I said. He laughed again. "What company?" he asked. "I'm not employed by any coach firm. I have other interests and if you and I can get together there won't be any need for you to bother whether you've got a job or not." '

'And you took him at his word?'

'Dame Beatrice, I had no option.'

'But if you obtained the information about the merger merely by accident, could you not have told your board of directors and promised secrecy?'

'Well, only in a way was it by accident. I overheard part of a telephone conversation. *That* was accidental enough. I'd been invited to attend a board meeting because the drivers were asking for more pay and, not wishing to be late, I had got there well before time. Well, knowing the place, I had slipped into a sort of little kitchen where the typists brewed up and which opened out of the boardroom. Nobody saw me, because the meeting, as usual, was held out of office hours, so I guessed nobody would be about until the meeting began and I thought I would sit in the kitchen and have a quiet smoke. I had no idea anybody was in the boardroom until the telephone rang and was answered. Well, that's where I should have made myself known and not listened in, I suppose, but as soon as I realised what was being arranged I admit I listened and when the meeting was over I found myself thinking about what I'd heard.

'Of course, my own job was my first consideration. Nobody can blame me for that. I'd heard one or two names mentioned and I knew they were younger men than myself, but my own name had not come up. It isn't easy to get another berth when you've been in management and are approaching fifty-five, so I thought I would try to find out exactly where I stood.'

'And that meant rifling the board's private files, I suppose.'

'You can't blame me. I only wanted to *know*.'

'And what you found out by your burglarious exploit was not conducive to your peace of mind, I take it.'

'No. There was nothing absolutely definite, you understand, but there was a pile of correspondence which, when boiled down to essentials, indicated to me that I could prepare myself for redundancy and that the most I could hope for was a very moderate golden handshake.'

'So when Vittorio put his proposition to you, you were ready to fall in with it.'

'Dame Beatrice, I was *obliged* to fall in with it. You see, I'd slipped into the little kitchen place again when the meeting was over, and then I'd gone back to the board room. When I'd found out what I could I ran straight into one of the stenographers. I recognised her at once as the girl who had been present taking down what was said at the board meeting. "So we had a good old rummage among the files, did we?" she said. "The cleaner saw you, you know. She thought you were entitled to be there, but, of course, I know better. So what are you going to do about it, Mr Honfleur?"

'Well, I did my best to keep my end up. "I have a perfect right to inspect the files," I said. "I am a member of the board." It didn't work, so I asked her what her price was. She giggled. "Higher than you can pay," she said. Of course it wasn't until I had this drink with him, that I found out she knew Vittorio. After that, there was nothing for it but to go his way.'

'And how long ago was this?' Dame Beatrice asked.

'About two years. Long before you and Miss Mendel came to dinner.'

'The merger is taking a long time to reach its climax, then.'

'All sorts of problems have had to be ironed out. If I'd realised how slow the whole business was going to be, I might have taken a chance and said I'd see Vittorio at the devil before I'd come in on his racket, but I thought it would only be a matter of months — even weeks — before the thing became a *fait accompli* and I, most likely, would then be out of a job.'

'But you are a free man. I mean, you haven't got a wife to worry about,' said Laura. 'That must surely make a difference.'

'Alimony,' said Honfleur, 'and also what is euphemistically known as "a little nest" to keep feathered. I wasn't sitting pretty, I assure you, or I would never have given in. Of course, it was the use of our coaches he wanted, to move the stolen antiques to the port of embarkation.'

'Well, B. Honfleur — and B. doesn't only stand for Basil — seems very sorry for himself,' said Laura, 'but I can't say I feel much sympathy for him. He seems to have behaved like a rather depraved ninny throughout the proceedings, wouldn't you say?'

'We still haven't heard the true story.'

'Even if (as I firmly believe) Vittorio stabbed those two drivers, help would have been needed in transporting the bodies, especially in hoisting them up to those gatehouses,' said Laura. 'Do you think Honfleur was the other man?'

'Time, as always, will show.'

'We still haven't actually put a name to the person who sneaked into the Stone House that night and bashed that dummy you'd had the forethought to slip into your bed. *That* couldn't have been Vittorio. He was dead. Besides, I thought we both recognised him, although we couldn't prove it.'

'You yourself pointed out, if you remember, that whoever it was must have had an acquaintance with the house. As we would scarcely imagine that any of our own relatives and friends would make an attempt on my life, there can be little doubt which two people come under suspicion, although, as you say, we have no proof.'

'So far as I can see,' said Laura soberly, 'the only people who could have been involved are Conradda Mendel and Basil Honfleur. Both had been to the house several times for psychiatric treatment and the room you used at that time as a temporay clinic was next door to your bedroom. Did you ever show Conradda into the bedroom?'

'No, but on her own confession the fact that she is not shown into bedrooms does not deter her from inspecting them.'

'But you don't really suspect Conradda Mendel, do you?'

'Women have done people to death before now.'

'But she'd had an operation. She was still convalescent, and it struck me that she was still looking pretty groggy when we called on her.'

'True. Ah, well, let us turn to other matters.'

'Back to Basil Honfleur, perhaps? Anyway, we know now how Vittorio came to have him under his thumb. We also know that Vittorio sometimes travelled on the coaches. What we *don't* know is whether he travelled on Noone's coach to Hulliwell Hall and on Daigh's coach to Dantwylch.'

'I am sure he travelled on neither. What is more, I have no doubt that when those two coaches, on their different days, set off, the deaths of the drivers were already planned. That planting of the bodies on the gate-houses was no haphazard or makeshift arrangement. It must have been most carefully worked out.'

'Do you think Honfleur, when he was checking up on hotels and such, travelled by coach, then?'

'Oh, I am sure he did not. That brings me to another point, and one which involves a fast car.'

'Honfleur's?'

'Very likely.'

'A fast car which took the loot from where it had been stored in a suitcase in the boot of the coach and carried it to Fishguard to be shipped to Eire, you mean.'

'Not necessarily into Eire, you know. There is one aspect which intrigues me and has puzzled me a little.'

'But now you know the answer?'

'Possibly. Possibly not. Did you ever wonder why Honfleur, under the name of Carstairs, bought a bungalow at Saighdearan?'

'No, I never thought of it, but, then, I wasn't connecting Honfleur with Carstairs.'

'We thought at first that a Welsh port was being used,' Dame Beatrice went on, 'but my suspicions were aroused when I realised that leaving the coach at Swansea was a blind. I thought of Fishguard, but I still was not quite satisfied. The bungalow at Saighdearan clinched the matter.'

'Oh! Stranraer to Lorne!' said Laura. 'And the stolen antiques were stored in the bungalow until they could be transported. Rather a long hop from Saighdearan to Stranraer, but I suppose your theory of a fast car still holds good, or, of course, they may have shipped the stuff down Loch Linnhe by boat to Oban and then on.'

CHAPTER 16

Confession of an Avenger

'Do you intend to find that out?' Laura went on.

'There is no need. I know most of what I need to know. What I do *not* know is who killed Vittorio. I can guess, but I cannot be certain. I have taken one step which may help. I have suggested to the police that it might be as well to make certain that the blood-stains on the bedding did actually come from the knife-wound on Vittorio.'

'I remember you suggested that to the inspector, but where else could they have come from?'

'His killer, as I also suggested. Please note that this time I do not say his murderer.'

'You're sticking to that idea about a fight and Vittorio getting the worst of it?'

'It is a possibility which ought to be examined.'

'A pretty long shot, surely?'

'Granted.'

'But I've always thought Vittorio was attacked as he lay in bed.'

'In his surprisingly large pyjamas and his socks and shoes?'

Laura stared at her employer.

'And the room turned upside-down,' she said slowly, taking in a new idea. 'Wrecked, you think, in a fight?'

Dame Beatrice did not answer the question. She said,

'Once I can establish the identity of Vittorio's killer, it will leave me free to conduct an awkward and embarrassing enquiry which I have known for some time I shall need to make.'

'Sounds like another investigation into the doings of Basil Honfleur.'

'Exactly, and this time without his co-operation and assistance.'

'Dirty work at the cross-roads?'

'I fear so. However, these unpalatable tasks have to be faced. My only respite will be the interval between now and the receipt of information from the forensic branch of the Scottish police.'

'But what gave you the idea that the murderer (I'm still going to call him that) could also have been wounded? Do you think that accounts for the gash on Knight's neck? How on earth did he manage to stab Vittorio in the back, then?'

'He had probably learnt some tricks during his Commando training. But never mind that. Those pyjamas have always been a puzzle to me. Vittorio was what I believe you would describe as a dressy little man. Those pyjamas were at least three sizes too large for him.'

'So what do you think really happened?'

'I can only surmise. Let us suppose that Vittorio broke into the house, probably by the same means as you did. He knew Carstairs (Honfleur) was not there so he inspected the rooms. Unknown to him, somebody had followed him, somebody for whom he had already made enquiry at the hotel, only to be mis-informed of the driver's name and coach company by the suspicious stripling Wullie.'

'So Knight killed Vittorio, and all that stuff about the two masked men was so much blah!'

'Please remember that my reconstruction is hypothetical. I have suggested one more thing to the police, that they search for Vittorio's own clothes. If I am right, there should be a tear in the shirt and jacket and both should be bloodstained. I think his killer undressed the body, put on to it the only pyjama trousers available . . .'

'Those would have been Carstairs' – or, rather, Honfleur's – as the bungalow belonged to him.'

'I imagine so. Knight did not put Vittorio into the pyjama jacket, possibly because he realised it had not a tear in it . . .'

'Why didn't he make one?'

'He may have thought it might come in the wrong place in the fabric.'

'But if they had a fight when both were fully dressed, how did the bloodstains, whichever man they belonged to, get on to the bed?'

'Presumably because part of the fight took place with both men rolling on it. The room was not a large one and the bed occupied more than half of it.'

Dame Beatrice, accompanied by her suite (as Laura put it), called at Basil Honfleur's office without warning and asked to see him.

'Oh,' said his secretary, 'I'm sorry, but he isn't here. I haven't heard from him since he left just after you called last time, so I suppose he's still in Bristol. That's where he said he was going.'

'Oh, never mind,' said Dame Beatrice. 'I expect you can help me. Is Driver Knight back on duty?'

'No, he's reported sick again. That knock on the head and a nasty gash in his neck have upset him, and no wonder.'

'I suppose you have to keep a record of the drivers' schedules.'

'Oh, yes, they have to be logged and any comments written against them.'

'Such as their getting murdered, perhaps.'

The girl, taken by surprise, gave a terrified little giggle and then blushed and stammered out:

'Well, I wouldn't put it like that. I should just put, "Killed in the course of duty," like as though it had been an accident. It looks better – not so crude.'

'So it does. Are you in sole charge of this office when Mr Honfleur is away?'

'This time I am.'

'What about those times when he goes off on his travels to inspect hotels or select new ones, or to investigate passengers' complaints?'

'Oh, well, it doesn't happen all that often, but I log it sort of unofficially in case anything goes wrong and I have to notify the board.'

'But you are now in sole charge of this office?'

'Well, I suppose you could call it that, although still responsible to Mr Honfleur and the board, of course.'

'Of course. But this time you are not responsible to anyone but yourself.'

'I don't know what you mean.'

'I wondered whether perhaps this time Mr Honfleur did not travel upon the company's business, but on some private errand of his own.'

Again the girl looked uncomfortable, but she did not giggle. She said,

'It's a confidential matter and I don't give away Mr Honfleur's business to anybody except the board.'

'Admirable, and, of course, I have no wish to pry. My errand was to ask where I could find Driver Knight.'

'Well, I suppose he's at home, unless he's gone into hospital. I haven't heard, not since he sent in another medical certificate.'

'But you know his address?'

'Oh, yes, I've got it somewhere.'

'And you know that I am empowered by your board of directors to look into the extraordinary things which have been happening, two drivers murdered and another viciously attacked – or so he claims.'

'Oh, yes. I'll find Knight's address for you. Do you wish me to ring him up and warn him to expect you?'

'Just as you think best, but it is hardly necessary.'

'Very well, then, I won't bother, although all our drivers are on the 'phone. They have to be.' She went over to a filing cabinet.

'And will you ask Mr Honfleur to ring me as soon as he gets back? He knows the number,' said Dame Beatrice, when the girl had written out Knight's address for her.

'I thought you meant to take Honfleur on the hop when he gets back,' said Laura, as they drove to the address Dame Beatrice had been given,

'The police will do that. I do not think Basil Honfleur intends to return to his office.'

'What makes you think that?'

'Certain remarks which you yourself let fall at our last meeting with him.'

'Don't tell me I let some cat or other out of some bag or other!'

'To an innocent man you would not have done so, but Basil Honfleur is anything but an innocent man.'

'Why, what did I say? Have I gone and put my foot in it?'

'Far from it. If Honfleur has absconded it makes my unpleasant task just a little easier. You asked him, if you remember, whether he wanted the word "amenities" spelt with one *m* or two.'

'I was only kidding.'

'You surprise me. I would have thought (as I'm sure *he* did) that you were expressing complete disbelief in his story and considerable contempt for him as a liar. You followed this later by tempting him into a confession that, far from being a free man and a blameless bachelor, he was paying alimony to a discarded wife and was also keeping a mistress. The reasons for his illicit enterprises were thus laid bare. If he was not to keep his employment – and he felt that his prospects were extremely poor once the long-projected merger went through – he had to find another source of income. To be an unemployed bachelor is one thing. To support two homes is another.'

'Wasn't Honfleur ever a genuine collector of antiques, then?'

'I hardly see how he could afford to be. I think that, if we were ever to visit his house again, the Welsh dresser and its dishes, including mine, would be gone and, bit by bit, the far more valuable objects which Conradda saw in Honfleur's bedroom. She managed, I think to see a hoard which was due to be stored at Saighdearan.'

'So how much of Honfleur's story is true?'

'It hardly matters. Now for Knight.'

'How shall you tackle him?'

'By telling him what I believe to be the truth and getting him to confirm it and to add such embellishments in his own defence as may seem good to him.'

Knight still wore a bandage round his neck. He did not seem in the least surprised to see them, although he looked a little suspiciously at their private-eye, the burly, ex-policeman escort.

'You were expecting us?' Dame Beatrice blandly enquired.

'They've just 'phoned up from the office,' Knight replied, 'to say you were on your way. What can I do for you *this* time?'

'Well, I venture to suggest that you tell me the truth, unless you prefer to have me tell it to you. May we sit down?'

'Sure. How much do you know?'

'Everything except your motive in killing Vittorio.'

'Motive for that?' He still kept a wary eye on the private detective who had taken a modest chair near the door. 'I see you've got a dick with you.'

'An unofficial one. He is not here to caution you or to inform you that you are not obliged to speak, but that, if you do, what you say will be taken down in writing and may be given in evidence.'

'He isn't a dick? You could have fooled *me*!'

'He is an ex-policeman, a retired sergeant. He has no connection with the case of the murdered coach-drivers. An attempt was made upon my life a short time ago, so he is here merely in the capacity of bodyguard to an elderly and enfeebled old lady.'

She leered hideously at Knight, who said nervously,

'Oh, that's all right, then.'

'Well, now, as my secretary would say, let's get on with it, shall we?'

'What do you expect me to say?'

'Well, not quite what you said before. Let us forget this colourful story of an attack, a black man and a kidnapping.'

'There *was* an attack.' He unwound the bandage on his neck. 'Take another look at that, if you don't believe me.'

'I accept the knife-wound on your neck. Let me replace the bandage. There! You had it from Vittorio, of whom you then got the better and killed.'

'It was in self-defence.'

'I accept that, too. Need you have killed him, though?'

'Well, he killed my two mates, didn't he?'

'He may have done, but my deductions indicate that, although he was an accessory to those murders, his was not the hand which struck the lethal blows.'

'Who did, then?'

'Never mind that, for the moment. Let me hear your own narrative, please.'

'All right, then, but, once again, how much do you know?'

'Enough to check your veracity. Of that you may be sure.'

'I've only your word for it.'

'Quite.'

This agreeable concession appeared to disconcert Knight. To cover this, as well as to hide his not over-clean shirt, he moved across the room, picked up a tweed jacket from the back of a chair and put it on.

'Stay sitting,' said the ex-police sergeant. Knight returned to his place and looked apprehensively at Dame Beatrice.

'Where do you want me to start?' he asked. 'But no taking things down in writing,' he added quickly, 'else I'm not talking.'

'Fair enough,' agreed Dame Beatrice. 'It will all come out in court, I daresay.'

'In court?'

'Of course. What you have to decide is whether you prefer to be tried for a killing in self-defence or for wilful murder.'

Knight half-rose. The impassive guardian at the door followed suit. Then both men resumed their seats, Knight with a half-inaudible expletive which he quickly smothered.

'It won't help me if I tell the truth,' he muttered. 'You can't get the better of the cops. It's like the income tax. They got the whip-hand of you the whole bloody time. All right, I better out with it, but I don't call it murder, mind you. I done Vittorio because I thought he done my mates. If it wasn't him, who was it?'

'Mr Honfleur, alias Carstairs.'

'Him? But he was in my push in the war!'

'Yes, I suppose he was in a Commando unit, as you told me you were. Both of you have turned your knowledge to a use which was never intended by those who trained you.'

'What's the difference between knifing Jerry sentries and knifing a dirty, thieving, double-crossing, blackmailing little wog?'

'In law and in time of peace the difference is substantial, but let us have your story.'

'Damn it all, why should I?'

Dame Beatrice shrugged her thin shoulders.

'In order to obtain, through me, the best defending counsel in England or Scotland,' she replied, 'so stop wasting my time. Tell me, first of all, what you know about the trade in stolen antiques.'

'None of us knew much about that,' said Knight, reassured by what appeared to be a change of subject. 'I reckon we all thought some sort of fiddle was going on, but it was no business of ours and everybody fiddles nowadays — you got to — so what?'

'Some sort of fiddle, as you call it, in this case refers to a series of well-organised and very remunerative thefts which the police have been following up for months. The valuables were stolen by the knowledgeable Vittorio and disposed of through the County Motors coach organisation. Unfortunately for themselves, Noone and Daigh became involved (accidentally, I'm sure) then perhaps they refused to co-operate; anyway, they were liquidated, one in Derbyshire, the other in West Wales. Your board of directors called me in to investigate. My secretary and I found the bodies, as you probably know.'

Knight was silent. Dame Beatrice waited, her sharp black eyes on her victim. Laura tried to read the titles of the books and paperbacks in a small glass-fronted bookcase on the wall opposite to where she was sitting. The bodyguard studied an evil-eyed stuffed seagull in a glass case.

'Look,' said Knight at last, 'this wog. Do you mean it wasn't him that done Noone and Daigh? They were stabbed, so it said in the papers, and Eye-ties are reckoned to be handy with a knife.'

'So are Commando troops, ' Dame Beatrice reminded him. 'The man who broke into my home was carrying a Commando knife. He dropped it in his flight.'

'So who do you reckon that was?'

'I know who it could not have been. It could not have been Vittorio, for he was already dead, and by your hand.'

'No, but he could have stabbed my two mates. He wasn't dead then.'

'Tell me, Mr Knight, if you had been on a tour (as driver of it, I mean) and Vittorio had asked you to move your coach while your passengers were sight-seeing, would you have obliged him?'

'No, nor a dozen like him.'

'Suppose another coach-driver had made the same request?'

Knight looked dubious. He had a long, melancholy face. This, and the bandage round his neck, gave him the lugubrious expression of a captive bird of prey.

'Well,' he said, 'if it was one of our own chaps and he wanted a bit of help I suppose I'd oblige if I could, but it couldn't be like that, you see, because we never only send the one coach at a time to any particular hotel or place, so the answer's a lemon.'

'You would not help the driver of another coach company, then?'

'Why should I? They got their own headquarters to 'phone up to if they find theirselves in trouble.'

'Yet it seems certain that Noone and Daigh did move their coaches and, from what you have just told me, they must have been obeying an order or request from somebody they could scarcely refuse.'

'That 'ud be Mr Honfleur. None of us wouldn't do it for nobody else. We'd know it was all right, coming from him, because we'd know he'd take full responsibility.'

'Thank you, Mr Knight. That is my own theory. Now let me tell you the true story of how you came to kill Vittorio.'

Knight stirred uneasily.

'I don't know as I want to hear it,' he said. 'You seem to have got it all worked out. I done it in fair fight and I'll stand by what I done.'

'How did you know that Vittorio was in Saighdearan?'

'Mr Honfleur told me to pick him up there, him and a couple of suitcases. I thought nothing of it, being that most of us had had Vittorio on a tour some time or other, so when I knew my mates had been stabbed I reckoned they'd fell out with him about some of the fiddles as we all guessed was going on. Tales gets swapped around in a depôt and some of 'em, perhaps, don't lose nothing in the telling. I guess you knows how it is.'

'We may take it for granted.'

'Right. Well, Mr Honfleur put me on the Skye tour with orders to pick up Vittorio, like I said. He told me Vittorio had a key to the bungalow and I was to meet him there after I brought the coach back from Skye. Well, you know the rest, I reckon, but there wasn't no murder. I fought fair and he fought dirty and I won. That's all there was to it. Still, when I knowed he'd croaked I stripped him like as though he'd been surprised by a burglar while he laid in bed, and then I lit out for home.'

'And it took you four days?'

'I hitched lifts and laid up at nights while I cooked up a story to tell Mr Honfleur, seeing I'd left my coach-party stranded and hadn't brought back no merchandise.'

'I am still not clear why you suspected Vittorio of being the murderer of your two comrades.'

'He was a wrong 'un, that's why.'

'An inadequate reason for suspecting him of murder. All the same, there is no doubt that he must have been an accessory after the fact. Well, now, Mr Knight, may I give you a piece of advice?'

'You said you'd find me a lawyer.'

'That is a promise I shall keep, of course. Meanwhile, you will find it to your advantage in the long run to give yourself up, confess to the fight and the killing and allow the police to take a sample of your blood. It *was* your blood on the bedding, was it not?'

CHAPTER 17

Sunset and Evening Star

'Well, he certainly gave away the fact that Honfleur and Carstairs are one and the same man,' said Laura.

'Unintentionally, I think. In any case, we knew they were the same, so the information, except as confirmation, is of no value.'

'He seems to have known all about that bungalow.'

'Oh, yes, he was a junior partner to Honfleur and Vittorio in the thefts and transport of antiques. There is no doubt about that. As you once pointed out – or was it I? – his illness, which lasted three weeks, seems to have been covered by only one medical certificate. I doubt very much whether we were told the truth about even that one. I think he was engaged upon business for Honfleur and Vittorio while he was absent from duty.'

'But his mates, the other drivers, would have known about that.'

'Doubtful, I think. It was in mid-season for the tours. I don't think any of them would have had leisure to pay him a visit and find that he was not at home.'

'Talking of the other drivers, I wonder why Noone and Daigh were the ones to be murdered?'

'They appear to have been indiscreet as well as unco-operative.'

'What makes you think so?'

'I received that impression from something two of the

passengers told us.'

'As when and how?'

'Well, Noone seems to have made a jesting remark to Mr Tedworthy which hinted that he sometimes carried more in the boot of the coach than his own and his passengers' luggage. He meant it only as a joke, but if it ever came to the ears of anybody with as sensitive a conscience and as much at stake as Honfleur that he had a jovial babbler among his drivers, he may well have thought that he would be better off without such a man.

'The same could apply to Daigh who, in making himself pleasant to Miss Harvey and Mrs Williams, mentioned that he was to pick up a girl-friend·*and her trousseau* in the car-park at Dantwylch. He had only to repeat this untimely jest to Honfleur when he joined him in the car-park that mid-day to seal his own fate just as surely as Noone may have sealed his.'

'We've yet to prove that Honfleur was absent from his office on both occasions, so that depends upon what the police can ferret out.'

'We have given them all the help we can.'

'Do you think Knight was gunning (or, rather, knifing) for Vittorio simply because he believed Vittorio had murdered his mates?'

'I doubt it very much. He had no proof that Vittorio was their murderer, so I think he was *also* (I give him *some* credit for mis-guided altruism) pursuing a long-standing vendetta of his own.'

'About what?'

'The likeliest thing is that it was about a woman, but we need not concern ourselves with that aspect of the matter.'

'So what's our next move?'

'I hardly think we need make one. The rest of the business may be left to the police. They will pick up Basil Honfleur sooner or later, Knight will either give himself up or be ap-prehended and I fancy he will furnish details of the shipments of stolen property. Incidentally, I think we may bid farewell to our faithful bodyguard. There is no possible danger for me now and I shall be glad to be freed from surveillance.'

'So we can settle down and get on with your book. I shall be glad of something peaceful and static for a change. We appear to have done nothing these last weeks but chase all over the kingdom. Talk about Land's End to John o'Groats!'

'You exaggerate. Besides, I have become accustomed to this roving life and should wish to continue it for a bit.'

'It's George's holiday next week, but I can take you anywhere you want to go.'

'Well, you may think it strange, but I have a great desire to take a coach tour.'

'*What*!'

'Yes,' said Dame Beatrice placidly, 'a coach tour would be delightful, and there is still time to book before the season ends.'

'And County Coaches goes into liquidation.'

'It is not going into liquidation. It is going to be merged with a greater and wealthier coach company, that is all.'

'With the result that it will lose its identity completely.'

'That is a sad thought. Rupert Brooke, if you remember, had a word to say about mergers, although he was referring not to coach companies but to the hereafter. He thought that there will be an end to kissing, when our mouths are one with Mouth.'

'Which tour do you want?' asked Laura, shortly, certain that she was being teased.

'We shall have to take what we can get so late in the season, but if there is a choice, I think I should like to re-visit the Yorkshire dales.' She passed a colourful brochure to Laura, who turned over the pages and studied the details of the Yorkshire tour. She soon tossed the booklet aside and asked:

'Is there enough evidence to get Honfleur convicted?'

'I think so. He will be identified by one of the attendants in the car-park at Dantwylch once his photograph is shown around by the police, and he will certainly be identified by the Whites.'

'I can't imagine why the Whites don't seem to have heard the rumpus when Knight and Vittorio had that scrap and wrecked the bedroom.'

'The bungalows are detached and I doubt whether the fight was as noisy as you think. There was no wardrobe to topple over and crash down and a good deal of the fighting seems to have taken the form of a wrestling-match on the bed.'

'What do you think happened to Vittorio's clothes?'

'I think the clothes have been wrapped around a boulder, tied on with string, and are now at the bottom of Loch Linnhe. You know, Laura, a pleasant thought strikes me. I should like to take up a hobby.'

'I thought your work was your hobby. Anyway, occasionally you collect things, although sooner or later you get rid of them.'

'You are thinking not of me but of Basil Honfleur, whose collector's mania led to his undoing. The acquisitive instinct, like most other instincts, shows a side of man's baser nature. One should not wish to accumulate.'

She waved a yellow claw at the collector's items she had received in exchange for her platters.

'Well, you've put Adam and Eve and the serpent behind you. What more do you want?' asked Laura.

'One should work with one's hands, as Adam and Eve did,' replied Dame Beatrice. 'When our coach tour is over, I think I shall carve a few love-spoons.'